Border Town

a novel

BORDER TOWN

a novel by
Hillel Wright

Printed Matter Press
Tokyo / New York

Border Town

Published by Printed Matter Press
Yagi Bldg. 4F, 2-10-13 Shitaya,
Taito-ku, Tokyo, Japan 110-0004

390 Mason Avenue
Staten Island, New York 10305

E-mail: info@printedmatterpress.com
http://www.printedmatterpress.com

in association with
SARU Press International
1169 Market St., Rm. 137
San Francisco, CA 94103-1521
E-mail sarupress@yahoo.com
http://sarupress.org

distributed in the United States
by Small Press Distribution
http://spdbooks.org

Cover image and illustrations by Taeko Onitsuka (2006)
Layout & design by Studio Z
Cover design by Joe Zanghi

A small portion of this novel was previously published in comix format in
MiNUS TiDES! Magazine as "Reborn to Raize Hell," story by Luke Warmwater
(Hillel Wright); drawings by Johnny Nemo (Daiv Pritchard)

First Edition

LCCN: 2006934425
ISBN 1-933606-08-8

Printed in Japan

Acknowledgements:

    I am most indebted to my Muse, Shiori Tsuchiya, without whose inspiration this book would not have been written.

    I would also like to thank Aurelio Asiain, Georgia Borcic, Kevin Brook, Kazuo Domon, "Dr. Ed", Norman Finkelshteyn, Wally Gagne, Ernest Hekkanen, Wayne (Elijah) Juhala, Harumi Katsumata, Rieko Kemi, Hideko Matsuura, Saki Miyagawa, Kathy Murphy, Alexandra Ogura-Kremer, Taeko Onitsuka, Daiv Pritchard, Donald Richie, Drew Stroud, Yoshie Terayama, Atsuko Ueno, Michael Woligrosky and Joe Zanghi, as well as the generous souls who read and commented on the manuscript or provided peaceful work-spaces in Hawaii and Japan where I could write.

Note on the text - Romanization and pronunciation of Japanese words

Japanese vowels are all pronounced individually and always with the same sound:

a as in *ma* and *pa*
e as in *hey* and *grey*
i as in *Mimi* and *Fifi*
o as in *hope* and *dope*
u as in *enthusiastic* and *exuberant*

In words with the double vowels *aa*, *ii* and (rare) *uu*, both vowels are voiced: ob*aa*san (grandmother) = *o-ba-a-san*; *ojiisan* (grandfather) = *o-ji-i-san*, while *obasan* (aunt) = *o-ba-san* and *ojisan* (uncle) = *o-ji-san*.

Since the double vowels *ee* and *oo* suggest to Western readers the sounds of *keep* or *creep* and *hoop* or *snoop*, this text will print such words with a single *e* or *o*. Thus, Osaka, not *Oosaka* and *besuboru* (baseball) not *beesubooru*.

When the vowels "ie" appear together, both are voiced, so the Japanese name *Marie* is pronounced Ma-ree-ay with equal stress on each syllable and not Ma-ree with the accent on the 2nd syllable as in the English name Marie.

The name of the character Fumie then, is pronounced Foo-mee-ay with equal stress on each syllable. It does not therefore, rhyme with *roomy* or *gloomy*.

The Silver Surfer, Marvel Comics

"I wouldn't brag about being cool in Tokyo...Mickey Mouse is cool in Tokyo."
—Lou Keester, *King of the Monsters; Godzilla Then and Now*

*for my good friends Oedipa & Mucho Maas,
my broker Mike Fallopian, my lawyer Manny DiPresso,
my guru Genghis Cohen and my agent Emory Bortz—
and a tip of the hat to their creator, Thomas Pynchon*

Happiness

"I know a good place to find baseballs," the Old Man said to the boy.

Although most people who saw them walking along or on their way to and from the Tama River bank, on the Kawasaki side, just across the river from Tokyo, thought of them as grandfather and grandson, the Old Man was actually the boy's father and he was really not so old, but had a good 45 years on his seven-year-old son.

The good place to find baseballs was a small, off-the-beaten-path river beach which led to and terminated in a miniature thumb-shaped peninsula which would, if the Old Man were an eagle flying 1000 meters overhead, look like the North Kohala district on the Big Island of Hawaii. A miniature inlet led around one side of the thumb to the beach, while the Tama River rushed by on the other. At the head of the mini-inlet, washed up on the micro-beach, was the astounding flotsam of modern Tokyo...a deflated rubber boat, black and gray...an assortment of oranges and grapefruit in various states of freshness or decay...fluorescent green tennis balls...a scarlet plush four-seat sofa, or couch or Chesterfield, depending on whether the chuckers had perhaps been Brits, or Yanks or Canucks and not Japanese...a black, clear-plastic-visored motorcycle helmet...and baseballs – lots and lots of the floatable Japanese style, hardball size rubber "softballs", which are thrown overhand at full speed in games at all levels of Japan's non-professional baseball leagues.

"So you and your friends are starting to play *yakyu* are you?" the Old Man asked.

"*Hai*...I mean yeah," the boy answered, "but no one calls it *yakyu* any more *otousan* – I mean Dad – we just call it *besuboru*."

Ah, language. Just this morning his wife Fumie, who no one mistook for the boy's *obaasan*, had called him a vacuum cleaner. Well, he thought he'd heard her say *soujiki* or "vacuum cleaner" to him as he was descending the stairs from their 2nd floor dwelling of a two-story duplex to go to work. When he got home that afternoon and asked her about it she laughed and said she'd been teasing him. What she'd actually called him was something like an "old fart"...*kusojiji* – literally a "shitty old man."

The Old Man and the boy discovered that the red sofa was made of foam rubber, which of course explained how it'd been able to float down the Tama River to this absurd little beach at the head of this crazy miniature inlet – "Baseball Beach." At least 25 baseballs, 15 day-glo yellow tennis balls and one regulation-size stitched leather Western style softball, bigger and fatter than the Japanese rubber "softball", the kind which is pitched underhand at full or half or whatever arc, speed or angle is determined by the relevant league, were floating in the shallow water or washed up on the beach.

The Old Man lit his little pipe for a puff or two.

The boy captured the softball which was still floating in the shallows with a long, broken-off piece of 1x2. While the Old Man smoked, the boy brought the ball over to the river's edge and wiped the pale, yellow-green scum of algae off the ball as best he could in the cold, clear winter river water. They also found a faded orange plastic box. On opening it, by turning down the hard plastic snaps, they discovered that it was lined with white Styrofoam – a floating mini-cooler.

They put the softball inside the cooler and snapped it shut then easily flipped over the lightweight red, foam rubber sofa and scraped off the mud, leaves and worms from the black bottom of the Chesterfield with an old, diagonally cut piece of drift bamboo. The winter sun and cold, dry air would do the rest. They stashed the cooler under the angle of the upturned couch.

*   *   *

The young woman was the boy's mother and the Old Man's wife. He was, in fact, in his fifties and she was not yet thirty and the boy was seven...but forget the math. She had trained to be a massage therapist in Seattle, where they first met ten years earlier, she an engrossed young student, he an engorged old geezer who she, however, saw as a dashing, romantic "Older Man", one on the edge of some dangerous endeavor more than likely, and a foreigner to boot – that is to her, being Japanese, even the American in his own native city was a foreigner.

He took her driving in his European car out of the rain forest and into the high, dry plateau of Eastern Washington. They rented horses and rode for three glorious, exuberant hours through the chaparral. Even the hours of pain and soreness afterwards didn't dampen her enthusiasm for the outing or her passion on the sagging box spring under the mattress in the cheap off-the-two-lane-blacktop motel room. After that, whether he knew it or not, she would never really let him go. Whether she knew it or not, perhaps no one will ever know.

*   *   *

The next time the Old Man and the boy visited Baseball Beach, they found the red foam rubber Chesterfield just as they had left it, upside-down, muddy bottom drying in the hard Tokyo winter sun. The softball, however, was lying next to the orange mini-cooler under the eave of the up-turned sofa's arms.

Was it magic, human communication, random action or distortion of remembered facts? Perhaps no one will ever know.

The Old Man decided to bring the softball home. The boy readily agreed.

*   *   *

The young woman's name was Fumie Akahoshi and she worked in a massage clinic in the small Kawasaki town of Shin Maruko. Shin Maruko served as a bedroom community to a number of huge high-tech companies which inhabited mighty high-rise office towers in the re-claimed marsh lands that were Kawasaki City's share of the Tama River flood plain, the silicon valley of suburban Tokyo.

The clinic was *wayo sechu*, a mix of Western and Japanese practices, offering traditional shiatsu massage as well as its Chinese ancestor *jin shin do*, Swedish therapeutic massage, and even Western re-interpretations of Japanese technique such as *reiki*. Fumie's three years of study in Seattle gave her the expertise and the edge that made the clinic stand out – discreetly – from the numerous small, narrow, crowded, liniment-smelling salons and *kurinikku* which dotted the area around the train station and down the cobble-stoned shopping streets which radiated out from the tiny station which served only one short-run local train. The short run, however, was between Yokohama station and Shibuya, a major terminal in central Tokyo.

The town crept down a slight gradual incline to the Tama River's west bank, still tidal under the Maruko Bridge, flowing into and ebbing out of Tokyo Bay. Just north of the railroad bridge into Tokyo, which was itself just north of the Maruko highway bridge, was a dam, the Chofu *seki*. On the east bank of the river were the fashionable and exclusive communities of Tamagawa-en and Den-en-chofu, the latter generally acknowledged to be the wealthiest neighborhood in Tokyo.

On the Kanagawa Prefecture side, Shin Maruko was known as "the poor man's Den-en-chofu," as much for its charms as its pretensions. Fumie's place of employment squeezed into this eclectic little commercial district behind a cornflower blue and yellow faux Swedish flag motif storefront and a sign both in English and *katakana* Japanese which read "Stockholm Massage" (*Sutokuhomu Massaji*): "The Swedish Touch."

*   *   *

She was a happy child. At least she'd been a happy child for about the first twelve years of her life. She grew up in a small city in Central Japan, the Tokai District, the Pacific Ocean side or east coast of the main island of the archipelago, Honshu. The city was in a river valley and the river was a source of fine clay, and so the city was traditionally famous for its pottery.

The river was also the home of the *ohsanshouo*, the elusive giant salamanders of Japan, as well as of the *ukai* fishing, where the *u* - or diving black cormorants fished for their human controllers. As Fumie grew older she sometimes went with her parents and younger brother to see the birds dive by torchlight on the river, metal rings around their necks to keep them from swallowing the fish they captured, causing them instead to deliver them to their masters in their low wooden boats.

The giant salamanders she saw only in her imagination, or perhaps in a splash near the river bank and a glimpse of a black amphibian tail swirling the surface as it, like its black-feathered cousin the cormorant, dove for the river bottom and its targeted prey. Or maybe that was her imagination too. She never really knew for sure nor, if truth be told, was this knowledge her desire. She was happy just to keep the intriguing mystery alive.

But the river was a dangerous place for a young girl to play beside, except under the watchful eye of her parents, or at least her mother, as her father usually used such events as cormorant watching or cherry blossom viewing or the summer high school baseball tournament to get drunk. Akahoshi-*sensei*, fortunately, was a happy drunk, not given to meanness, foul moods, brooding silent depression or violence. But neither was he much taken with watching after his young offspring or taking much time to pay attention to them. He worked as a respected acupuncturist and, given the serious nature of his work and the care and attention required to build and protect his reputation – and by logical progression his income – he was very much inclined during those few hours in the week when not engrossed in the stresses and demands of his profession, to spend them in watching baseball, in drunkenness or in sleep.

So the young Fumi-chan spent her leisure hours which, compared to her father's were many, in the shallow waters of the rice fields or the tiny creeks and waterways that served them. There she would hunt for all manner of amphibious life forms – frogs, newts, crayfish and small freshwater crabs. At first she would bring them home in little plastic boxes filled with water, but after witnessing – and crying over – their eventual deaths a time or two too many, she gave up this practice and merely captured them, stroked their smooth wet skins or shells, rhythmically rubbed their exposed bellies and, satisfied that she had communicated her love for them to their primitive amphibian or crustacean brains, and likewise satisfied her need for living things to notice her, to focus and depend on her, she would set them free in the murky shallow waters from whence they came.

*　　　　*　　　　*

She was happy during her hours in the wet rice lands, with the powder blue sky above her and the *kosagi*, the white rice field egrets, softer and whiter than the clouds, off about their business, mirrors to her own fertile imaginings of herself. Like her, they stalked and captured the tiny creatures of the paddies, but being driven by hunger, or perhaps habit, they devoured them. She, on the other hand, put their fate in her hands and offered them love.

She was happy riding her bicycle alone along the quiet dirt roads between the rice fields, much happier than when riding with her few occasional friends along the bicycle course above the river. She was never quite comfortable in the company of other children, less so with adults, and quite fearful in the presence of crowds of strangers.

She was happy when her mother Akiko had time for her, when they would make *okonomiyaki* pancakes together in the cluttered kitchen of their old, but rambling wooden house. The house was big for its neighborhood, on the outer edge of the town, overlooking a gulch that plunged sharply just across the road to one of the swiftly running creeks that fed the big river and nourished both the giant salamanders and the rice paddies. It was a big dwelling, but also quite old and had once housed not only the family residence, but also the acupuncture clinic and its storerooms and offices, all of which had, some years before, in the early years of her father's practice, in fact before she was born, been moved into a more modern, concrete building in the city's rebuilt shopping district downtown. And so the kitchen was big, but crowded with things...many things.

Among the many things were the iron *nabe* pots and fry-pans, the bowls, plates, cups and other dishes, the dried or drying herbs, the pickled vegetables, the jars of dried, salted fish or dried seaweeds or mushrooms, the boxes of tea — both the traditional green teas of Japan and the exotic black and orange teas of China, India and the British Isles, and the jars and bottles of spices, tonics and old Chinese remedies.

She was happy to be left alone in the multifarious feminine world of the kitchen, to peer into mysterious containers to discover strange smelling powders and extracts and creams made from the bones or horns or organs of animals, or from fantastic and fascinating plants like the huge, humanoid giant ginseng root, which dominated the northwest corner of the kitchen, magnified into greater prominence by the preserving liquid in which it rested inside its enormous clear glass jar.

And she was also happy during those all too infrequent

moments when she helped *okaa-san* cut up the cabbage, the thin slices of pork and the white and purple tentacles of boiled octopus to mix in with the mung bean sprouts and the *okonomiyaki* batter.

*   *   *

She was happy, when at eight or nine or ten she was old enough to be trusted with the care of Tomohiko, her younger brother, who was five or six or seven, as they played in the tiny park across from their house, or in the large ten *tatami* mat room downstairs, across the hallway from the kitchen, or in summer, in the cool shade of the tall persimmon and broad plum trees which stood at the entrance to the flower garden in the crowded yard behind the house.

In many ways she was even happier when Tomo-*kun*, ever more outgoing and sociable than she, went out with his gang of neighborhood boys to the baseball field or on bicycle rides beside the rice paddies or on expeditions to catch, in fine mesh long-handled nets the *semi*, the chirruping cicadas of the long humid summer afternoons.

Cicadas or beetles or praying mantids or any of the dry insects – even butterflies – held little interest for Fumi-*chan*. She, instead, preferred the soft smooth wetness of the frog and crayfish bellies, or even the hard, solid, yet glaringly vulnerable undersides of the crabs. It was the shining wetness and exposed helplessness of these small wetland creatures that attracted her and to which she could apply her own special form of tenderness and compassion and love.

*   *   *

She was happy when she started junior high school and was introduced to the magic of the art room – the jars of dry pigments to be mixed with water, the colorful oils with all their wonderful names – burnt sienna, chrome yellow, cobalt blue – the large white sheets of drawing paper, the many and various brushes of differing lengths and shapes and degrees of stiffness or softness, the smells of turpentine, black India ink, acrylics and stretched canvas over frames of pine or yellow cedar.

She was happy when she could draw in her very own sketchbook, with charcoal or colored chalk or graphite pencil. First, the seasonal flowers – the delicate pink *sakura* cherry blossoms that were just beginning to bloom when school started in the spring, or the fading colors of the plum blossoms, their long reign of winter glory ending. Then the pale blue or purple hydrangea of the rainy season, the late roses when school began again after a short summer recess, the elegant white, violet and yellow chrysanthemums which grew to enormous size in autumn and the red camellias that kept color alive during the winter darkness.

Next she drew the birds – the darting, black-capped swallows which built their nests under the eaves of the school's roof; the big, ever-present jungle crows, with their enormous beaks; the wild ducks, which herded their newly hatched young along the backwater streams that fed the big river; the tiny, olive green *mejiro* with their famous white eyes, and even the common brown sparrows that flocked around the schoolyard daily, and the silky mourning doves that haunted the outer edges of the school athletic fields, feasting on beetles and worms.

At the last, she began to draw people – especially faces

and hands. Her mother, Akiko; her art teacher, Tanikawa-*sensei*, her best friends Mayumi, Megumi and Sanae. She was a happy child, at the cusp of womanhood.

*   *   *

But on returning to school in the spring for her second year of junior high school her happiness was abruptly shattered.

A new principal had come to the school, Takayama-*sensei*. He was a tall, sharp-featured man with narrow eyes beneath slick black eyebrows which seemed forever furrowed in displeasure. He walked with his spine straight, at a perfect right angle to the floor. Some said he was a Right-winger, a militarist, one of that noisy band of thugs that preached their nationalistic propaganda through ear-splitting amplifiers from ominous, square, black vehicles, protected by chain-link fencing in front of the railway station on Saturday afternoons.

At the very least, he was a strict traditionalist and his first act of authority was to cancel the art, music and drama classes and replace them with calligraphy, calisthenics and martial arts.

At first she was not so unhappy studying calligraphy which, after all, Japanese students must practice in order to learn the various syllabaries and pictographs necessary to read and write their language. She even felt a certain delight in perfecting her brush strokes for the Chinese *kanji* characters which made up her name – *fumi*...letter; e...picture.

But the only color of ink was black, the only permissible paper was a glaring white, and the teacher, Meguro-*sensei*, was strict and adhered forcefully to stringent, traditional forms.

For a martial art she chose karate. Its energetic forms

and movements allowed her to vent her anger and frustration at being pulled from the arts she loved and, hating failure above all else, she progressed slowly but steadily to black belt. But she never felt any love for this discipline and even though she was able to use it to reduce her stress, her practice never really made her happy

*   *   *

She couldn't remember being really happy again until she met the Old Man. She was in her late teens and he was in his forties. Now, looking back, she realized that, most likely, he didn't consider himself an old man when they'd met about ten years earlier in a big waterfront park in Seattle. It was a Saturday, a day off from the massage school she was attending days and the English language school she went to at night. She was drawing sea-birds with colored chalks in a large sketchbook. There were huge flocks of herring gulls, shoals of sea ducks, teals, grebes, a few large and majestically gliding loons, even a few black cormorants which reminded her of the birds diving for sweetfish on the big river of her hometown back in Japan.

He was watching the sea birds through a pair of heavy, old-fashioned high powered binoculars, and jotting down things in a small notepad. After a time she stopped sketching and shading and he approached her and asked if she'd like to look at the birds through his binoculars. She did. The binoculars were very powerful and she was fascinated by the mix of garish and subtle colors of the various ducks and their cousins, the grebes, loons and teals, and by the nuances of the gull wings as those raucous and unromantic birds carved graceful arcs, curves and circles in the pale blue sky.

Seeing the birds through the binoculars made her imagine she was seeing them through the Old Man's eyes, and because of this conceit on her part, the Old Man gained, albeit unbeknownst to him at the time, some of the romance, the grace, the beauty which belonged, naturally and rightfully, to the birds.

*   *   *

The small black, white and red bird caught the Old Man's eye instantly. Hawaiian birds were not always colorful and not often plentiful. So he took care to notice whatever birds he could and, if not possible to photograph them – he rarely carried a camera with him nowadays – to at least imprint them onto the memory boards inside his brain.

"Money talks" – one of the guys around the table, almost certainly tourists, not locals, was laughing, along with the rest of the guys and one wary woman, an elegant, young corn tassel blonde. But the laughing guy forgot to quote the rest of the equation... "bullshit walks." The Old Man turned his attention back to the bird and then to his notebook, feeling slightly guilty with himself for violating his self-imposed "Do nothing/Write nothing" year of exile away from Fumie and the boy.

The first thing a good beach does to you is make you want to take your watch off. What makes it a great beach is when you, in reality, really do take it off. He looked at what he'd written and emphatically added one more word. *Really!*

Then the small bird's antics on the wooden deck of the outdoor café claimed his attention again and he lost the thread of his neighbors' eavesdropped conversation.

"Well, I guess the same's true about a woman."

"Or a man."

"Or a man" he heard just before their laughter ended the conversation and they got up noisily and converged in front of the register to pay their bill.

*   *   *

What made the Old Man happy long before anything ever made him think of the term "Old Man" meaning anything other than the 100-year-old Italian who walked leaning on a silver-headed black wooden cane every morning in the summer down the gravel road past his grandmother's summer cottage – both his grandfathers had died before he was born – was the Beach.

He had learned the turn of the tides as a little boy in the heady days of prosperity following World War II on the Connecticut side of Long Island Sound, in and around the wide estuary of the Connecticut River, the great river of New England, where it emptied it's often muddy waters into the green mouth of the Atlantic Ocean, that gullet-like appendage and entrance to New York Harbor, Long Island Sound.

He knew only summer beaches – July and August – except for perhaps a rare spring-cleaning trip in early May, when he was old enough for, if not inclined toward, helping with the rougher, heavier chores like mowing the lawn in the weed-entangled empty lot which his grandmother owned but had not build on next to the cottage, or cleaning the gutters around the cedar-shingled roof from a tall, wobbly wooden ladder, or an exotic late September "winterizing" trip to put up storm windows and round up the gardening implements and put them in the converted outhouse now used as a tool shed.

But summer was the season he knew and loved the best, the season which most made him happy. Low tides, in summer, were for dragging a net in the channels between sand bars in an estuarial maze beyond the mouth of a small tidal stream known, quite accurately one might have imagined at the time, the Oyster River. In reality, the oysters were long gone. You could, however, catch literally bushels of blue-shell crabs, but that story rightly belongs to high tides.

Low tides were when you caught bait fish for the lobstermen for which you could be paid a large amount of lobster or a small amount of cash. It always seemed a shame to him that he'd been born into a Jewish family still kosher enough – the summer cottage was his Polish-born grandmother's – to refuse to allow shell fish like lobsters, crabs, clams or oysters or scale-less bottom-feeders like catfish or eels to be eaten in their home. They overlooked it, however, when he ordered fried clams with Tartar sauce at the Howard Johnson's on the highway, or at the local clam shack near the beach.

High tides were for swimming. But even though he loved to swim and became quite strong and good at it following a series of Red Cross and YMCA courses and lots of practice at summer high tides, his first love and what really made him happy was low tide.

"Oh boy, low tide!" he'd cry joyfully when his father's low-priced family car, usually a Plymouth or Ford, plain black without a radio, crossed the Oyster River bridge and he could see the state of the tide in the estuary.

Dragging between sandbars at low tide filled the net with a variety of sea creatures, mainly small schooling fish like the mid-water shiners and the bottom-dwelling mummychubs. Both of these were used as bait by the many food fishermen, mostly commercial lobstermen who went sport fishing – in reality, food fishing – with rod and reel after hauling and setting their traps in the early morning, or residents, both summer and year round who fished from the rocks and breakwaters or just off-shore in small boats.

The fish that bit were the two flatfishes – flounder and fluke – porgy, blackfish, Atlantic eels and snapper blues. You could dig for sandworms on the tidal flats too, and as a boy the Old Man had preferred them for bait when casting for flounder from the end of the breakwater of seaweed-curtained and barnacle-encrusted boulders and rocks.

Dragging became really exciting when you scooped a big school of the thin silver shiners or fat brown chubs...or when you caught two or three big blue-shell crabs which you could sell around the neighborhood if you put them, right away, to keep them fresh, into a galvanized iron bucket of saltwater with a handful of seaweed to give them shelter from the sun. You could do this if the crabs came near the end of the tide. Otherwise, you could admire them and later brag to your friends about it before letting them go. Sometimes you'd catch two crabs mating, the smaller male clinging like a vise to the larger female beneath him. He used the word "fucking" for the first time while describing this phenomenon to a female cousin. He mother overheard him and washed out his mouth with a bar of rough brown laundry soap.

Dragging could go for two or three hours, depending on the tide. He and his favorite fishing partner, Jimmy Higgins, always kept two of the 2-gallon galvanized buckets filled with seawater for the live bait catch, one for the shiners and one for the mummychubs because the shiners died faster and you didn't want dead fish in the live bait bucket.

The sand bars gradually disappeared as the tide came in,

so you went swimming. He loved swimming under water, even though his eyes turned red and bloodshot from the salt. He was very happy when, at last, at about age 11, he got a diving mask of real tempered glass, a proper black snorkel with a purge valve and a set of two-tone blue Voit adjustable diving fins. He made himself a spear gun out of a hot dog fork and some strips cut from a rubber inner tube and skewered one or two hapless sand-dabs and a couple of startled blue-shell crabs before giving it up, tired of the needless, wasteful deaths and, perhaps even more so, tired of an undersea terrain of endless sand.

The other boyhood activity which had made the Old Man happy was baseball. His happiest days were as a young sandlot player in his New England neighborhood, at ages seven, eight and nine . The boys on his block played stickball with a broom handle and a tennis ball or red rubber ball cut in half in the street after school, until dinner calls from their mothers or a warning from the patrolling policeman ended the game. If the days were long enough, the game picked up again after dinner.

Real baseball was played on the diamond of the elementary school during recess and after lunch, but it was seasonal, competing with marbles and kite-flying in spring and autumn and losing out completely to snowmen and snowball fights in the winter. In summer, when school was out and before his family left for a few weeks at the beach, or after they returned home, he and his friends played on a sandlot field about half a mile from their block, just across the town line. They had to cross a small apple orchard to get there and there were many stories about how the farmer had shot at boys stealing apples, with a shotgun loaded with rock salt. But since the apples were small and green during baseball season, this remained an urban legend, outside their own personal experiences.

The baseball diamond had an old backstop but no outfield fence. The base paths were trampled down often enough to keep weeds from growing and once every few weeks one of them would sneak off with his father's push-type lawnmower and they'd cut the infield and outfield grass. They chose up sides, either by tossing the bat and fisting up the handle, last fist below the knob the winner, or by "odds or evens" – shooting out one or two fingers from behind the back. He was never chosen either first or last. He was a good player but not a star. He'd play any position needed, except pitcher or catcher, although like most boys his age, he dreamed about being a pitcher and learning how to throw a curve. He could hit well, but not for power. He hit a lot of line drives, but never got homeruns.

His happiest moment was when they challenged a Little League team from the other side of the avenue which crossed their neighborhood. The Little Leaguers showed up wearing their uniforms, shouting encouragement to each other and going through a series of pre-game drills. His team threw balls around in the outfield, batted fungoes to the infielders and finally took a short batting practice. A couple of them roamed the edge of the outfield to look for balls hit into the high grass. Baseballs were expensive and scarce, so they couldn't afford to lose any. The Little Leaguers had brought a bagful, as well as real bases. They agreed to use the Little Leaguers' balls in the game.

He played first base in that game and later moved to right field. He got 3 hits in 5 at bats – two singles and a double and scored every time. He didn't make any obvious errors. In fact, every kid on the team played his heart out and they trounced the proud Little Leaguers 11 to 6. He went home that evening very, very happy.

The next year he tried out for the Little League again, and made a team after failing at ages eight and nine and for the next two seasons played less baseball than ever before. He was not a starter. He came in only as a pinch hitter in the late innings or as a substitute outfielder if his team was way ahead or way behind. First base, his preferred position, was won by Ronny Vincent, a remarkable one-handed player, a kid born with a shortened right arm with a tiny fist of stunted fingers at its end. Ronny was tall for his age and lanky, a natural athlete. He gloved throws to first with his mitt on his good left hand and in one seamless movement flipped the glove onto his right stump and threw the ball to the second baseman with his left, and the ball then went "around the horn" before returning to the pitcher. Ronny also made some memorable leaping snares of line drives, a foot or more above his head.

The regular outfielders were Dave Kovaleski in right field and his younger brother Mickey in left. Dave was their big homerun hitter and Mickey hit for average and stole bases. But the star of the team was the centerfielder, Ocell "Pops" Blocker, their own little league Willie Mays. Ocell led the league in batting average, RBI's, stolen bases, runs scored and fielding. He was the only kid in the league to play an entire season without making an error.

So the Old Man had a uniform, but not much to do, other than shout "No batter! No batter!" or "Hey pitcha, pitcha!" or "Little bingle! Little bingle!" from his seat on the bench. His most embarrassing moment, other than misjudging fly balls in the outfield, was when he singled against a tough opposing pitcher, but then knocked himself out sliding headfirst into the steel holding stake attempting to steal second base. He was happy when his parents moved to the suburbs the following year.

*   *   *

After finishing his coffee, he drove to the nearest beach. He found a picnic table and a fire pit and set up "camp" for the day. Facing his fire, he watched as the flames and smoke conjured up the tragic phantoms of his recent past. But soon enough, the coursing of the surf on the beach began to harmonize with the crackling of the mesquite and dry coconut husk beach fire. He was happy in moments like these.

The next morning he rose early and drove straight to the beach. He was happy to be the first person in the surf for the first time in thirty years. That too had made him happy, no doubt with a different perception in real time than in memory, thirty years ago.

*   *   *

She had been happy when her shamefully (to her) little titties grew into full, shapely globes following the birth of the boy, her first child. The Old Man had been happy too – who knows, maybe even happier than she – on account of this development.

It was around this time that the Old Man, greatly affected by the transformation of his wife from sprite to matron and of himself from rogue to patriarch, got the inspiration for what finally, a few years later, earned him his first small fortune by creating a concept and writing or co-writing several scripts for a daytime comic soap opera for Japanese TV called *We're No Angels*, based on the *Five Books of Moses*. The Three Patriarchs/Four Matriarchs segment of *Genesis*, especially the bits about Lot and his daughters and later Jacob and his two wives, Rachel & Leah, got blowout ratings when first aired and the show continued to reap massive royalties, having been translated into 31 languages and broadcast on various network, cable and satellite stations in over 60 countries in re-runs. After three seasons he moved on to the *New Testament*, changing the program's name to *We're No Saints*. The episode with Jesus flirting with the Samaritan woman at Jacob's well topped all previous records but he was happy when the series mercifully ended after two more long and increasingly tedious seasons in Japan. The idea of writing a soap opera had always been faintly embarrassing to him and the pressure of being funny on demand began to take its toll on his health, confidence and peace of mind. Although he couldn't have cared less about the re-runs, the royalties left him now, in his sixties, a man of some means whether he ever penned another preposition, particle or prevarication.

Fumie thus had no economic need to work while she stayed in a relationship with the Old Man. But she could never think of living her life that way – dependent on another's lucre – creating co-dependence in response. She'd seen too much of that all around her – aunts, friends, cousins, mother. "*Sho ga nai*" was what they said in Japanese. "Nothing can be done about it." She knew that kind of dependency would never make her happy.

Art

She became famous as a *manga* artist, the Queen of Japanese comix, but that was a few years later, after the Old Man...after the Old Man. She was never quite sure what had made her happy during those years. Well, maybe she was sure. She was only really happy while drawing the manga.

She was lucky to have realized her true artistic nature at a time when another Japanese trend was sweeping the globe, like the sports fans' wave sweeps a sold-out stadium. Manga – the Japanese style comic book, with its unique dramatic and symbolic lettering style, intelligent, adult-themed stories and seemingly endless series of episodes, adapted into English, or Russian, or French or Korean or Chinese, was becoming an international phenomenon just when Fumie Akahoshi's manga *Chibi Hanako-chan* (literally, Little Miss Flower Child) appeared and was carried along by the swelling tide.

What had started as her own private satirical war against the abuses of public trust perpetuated by charlatans in the "massage" business when a young masseuse, increasingly forced into more and more explicitly sexual acts at work, takes over the business from her quack of a boss, who she turns into her sex-slave and object of constant humiliation, and re-invents the clinic as a clandestine S & M and Bondage emporium, especially selected by wealthy perverts who send her their intended submissive (and usually unwitting) future sex-slaves under the guise of getting a therapeutic or recreational massage.

Chibi Hanako-chan's transformation from half-naïve, half-curious waif, straight out of massage school, to fast-thinking, tough-talking dominatrix, and the many levels of satire – political, cultural, social and sexual – that the series expressed, gave it a broad fan base – from the nine-year-old TV Girl Gang *anime* fans, who bought the trademark accessories, to the Professors of Art and Sociology and Literature who studied her works in special seminars at universities, to the young career women, *freeters* – the part-time working Japanese social rebels – and a seemingly random demographic of male readers, mostly in the 25-35 year old age group, consisting of both *otaku* – Japanese electronics geeks – and salarymen alike.

*　　　*　　　*

But first came the Old Man's art – at least the one which gained him his first 15 minutes of fame and some notoriety on the fringes of respectability – as either a guerilla artist – something akin to the graffiti tagger – or an advanced form of concept/environmental artist, who went around the river and ocean beaches of the Kanto plain creating what the Art world would call "assemblages" or "installations," but which he privately called "set-ups" and the media came to call "rooms," out of the vast storehouse of industrial and post-industrial waste which is daily abandoned on or floats up on the shores of Eastern Japan. He concentrated his efforts on the Pacific Ocean beaches of the Shonan district in Kanagawa Prefecture – Kamakura, Enoshima, Oiso – and on the shores of the great rivers of the Kanto plain, especially the Tamagawa, which divides Tokyo city and state from Kawasaki city and Kanagawa.

His other arts, and they were considerable in number if not in talent, had reserved him an outpost on the borders of the art world. He had originally, relatively late in life for the conventional "artist", found some degree of mainstream acceptance as a black & white photographer. After two or three failed attempts at a successful coffee-table book, he finally achieved a modest victory with a book of portraits of the denizens of Tokyo's bizarre fashion counter-culture in all their finery, from Goth and Center Guy, to Mountain Hag to Minnie Mouse, captioned with terse quotes from popular literature – song lyrics, TV commercials, comic books – or original three line poems which of course stirred up a flurry of cock-fighting among those who cared whether or not the author intended them to be read as haiku.

After a season of good reviews, a lot of free publicity in the media and a gallery show of the original photos, the book was out of print two years later and not re-issued. But building his set-ups or "Rooms" on the beaches from junk found washed up or floating became his meal ticket and credit card and after five years of at best anonymity and at worst hostile suspicion, he was now given a minor hero's welcome at small towns and communities all around East Japan which discovered they had a small beach somewhere within their official boundaries – on the ocean, the bay, a river or even a creek – which has too much garbage on it – an abandoned motorcycle and a couple of visored motorcycle helmets, a discarded sheet metal bar-b-q, an assortment of plastic *bento* lunch boxes, an obsolete cell phone, a chipped ceramic tea cup, some stray living room furniture washed up in a flood – and that they can be on NHK-TV and 5 local channels if they pay this crazy foreigner to make "art" out of it – the chair frame a body with a blue-black metallic helmet head having tea with a girl-body fashioned from a stripped down, washed out Fender Stratocaster guitar topped by an algae-etched soccer ball head, with other junk-formed figures reclining seductively on a red foam rubber flotsam couch.

And, as luck would have it, another global Japan-chic wave was just beginning to crest and the Old Man was able to ride the curl and, as the wave finally broke after a long satisfying but demanding ride, find himself looking back at it from the beach.

He, quite naturally, photographed all his "Rooms" and a series of three coffee table books of the photos were successfully promoted by a major New York publisher. The books were called: *Bare Rooms*, *Can-Did Camera* and *My Room*, none of the titles being the Old Man's choice. And after a while he became something of a joke, known among his various sets of friends, colleagues and associates as "the Room Man" – or worse – "Mr. My Room."

Disillusioned, he gave up photography once and for all and turned his head to a series of artistic endeavors for which he had absolutely no talent. These included pottery, music – trying to learn to play the trombone – modern jazz dance, and finally, poetry. But despite his failure to create a new career, he and his family were able to live a modest, middle-class lifestyle on his royalties, sales from his storeroom of file photos to various trade, travel and technical magazines, and, without doubt, on Fumie's salary at the massage clinic. That is, until Fumie got her shot at the limelight with *Chibi Hanako-chan* after he had struck oil with his concept for the Japanese TV series, *We're No Angels*.

*   *   *

The Chibi Hanako-chan character herself, who soon, naturally enough, became a TV and movie *anime*, and later a Game character, had the curious blending of an innocent elementary school girl – perhaps nine years old – with the grace and power of a ninja crossed with an Amazon. It wasn't until much later that she was given, by her creator, the psychic powers and abilities which got both of them into so much trouble. The most effective techniques in portraying the various aspects of the character were the sometimes subtle, sometimes radical alteration of the shape, coloration or shading of her eyes from frame to frame and the artist's skilful use of the various modes of Japanese lettering – or calligraphy – the feminine, cursive *hiragana*, the sharp, macho, angular *katakana* and the classic, sophisticated Chinese *kanji* characters.

There were, naturally enough, only so many corrupt massage clinic quacks whose sorry asses Chibi Hanako-chan could kick and only so many rich, homosexual, dominant male perverts with both the ¥en and the yen for such risky business to keep said business in business. So, as a matter of course, Chibi Hanako-chan evolves into a kind of free-lance Erin Brockavich shit-disturber and rabble-rouser with a generally (perhaps overly transparent) feminist bent – or should we say twist?

Story after story and book after book shows her taking on a panoply of Japanese social types – corrupt politicians, subway rush-hour gropers and grabbers, crooked business executives, doping athlete heroes, militarist goons, gay male fashion czars and finally, the manga story that catapulted her into international fame and national notoriety, the entire Imperial system, including that god-like personage – the Emperor himself. But all this came later, after the Old Man.

*   *   *

In the meantime, the boy, Ichiro, is in his late teens and near to completing his course at a prestigious international high school in Tokyo, the Old Man in his sixties but in his own mind not yet old. After five lucrative seasons which, however, peaked with the fourth, *We're No Saints* was cancelled and the Old Man breathed a sigh of relief and began contemplating retirement.

On the other hand, *Chibi Hanako-chan's* star is rapidly rising with the TV animation series now on air and the manga plowing inexorably through the ocean of Japanese pulp towards its – some would say – unavoidable and inevitable detente – its collision with that massive ethno-cultural iceberg, the Japanese Emperor.

The boy is planning to attend an American or Canadian university, either in Washington state or British Columbia. This was, after all, the neck of the woods in which his parents first met. In his childhood his parents were never more than almost famous and almost rich...perhaps you would have described them as "well-off" or "comfortable" or even "middle class," so the boy grew up rather unspoiled and with few pretensions, but also somewhat unmotivated, with few expectations for the future.

The Old Man is leaving Japan, the boy, his wife Fumie, everything, and going to live in a remote rural area of Hawaii Island for a period of one year. He has no plan to write other than to conscientiously *not* write, no plan to take photos, other than *not* to take photos, no plan to create, other than to *not* create, perhaps even to destroy.

He wants to give his aging brain and body a complete about-face, a complete rest.

He wants to eat a lot of fresh local fruit – avocadoes, papayas, red grapefruit,, oranges, all kinds of bananas, mangoes and passion fruit – and fish – *ahi, ono, onaga, opelu, aku, uhu* and *ulua* – in season. He plans to live off 1/4 of his royalties, leaving 1/4 each for his wife and their son with the last 1/4 put into a "retirement" fund, because he doesn't yet consider himself retired. The Old Man is simply gonna spend the year deciding whether to retire at seventy (which would leave him practically already retired) or to keep going until 80, considering this year a "sabbatical" and leaving him over a decade of "Art" left to go.

The woman is now completely caught up in her art. The boy would soon be on his way to Seattle or Vancouver or Hawaii – he'd decided to apply to the Hilo campus of U of H as well as the Universities of Washington and British Columbia and Simon Fraser University. With the Old Man gone and the manga and TV animation projects in full bloom, life was – in spite of the busyness, the hurry and the stress – good...very, very good. And getting better.

Or so she thought...or would have been thinking at the time. Until that nasty little run-in with the Japanese Imperial forces.

*   *   *

Meanwhile, during the first few months of his self-imposed Hawaiian exile, the Old Man had developed a secret agenda. He'd been plagued by a strange recurring dream in which he was visited – or perhaps "accosted" would be a better word – by his oldest son – not the boy, Ichiro, but the offspring of some ultimately casual, however passionate encounter from his hippie days. Perhaps even a one-night stand. In fact, as he looked back on it, the Old Man's sexual revolution had been a depressing series of one-night stands. He now wanted to search his memory and see if he could make a concrete connection with the past.

A redheaded cardinal boldly landed on his patio garden table and checked him out...calmly, carefully, especially for so small a bird. After a few seconds, in which the Old Man paid close attention to the details of the bird – his blood-red cap, black beak, leathery little yellow legs – the bird darted to the next table which was, like most of the courtyard, empty, chirped once and then took flight and disappeared into the branches of a *keawe* tree.

*   *   *

He was now more than halfway through his year of write-nothing/do-nothing, his year of isolation and intro-spection. Except for the haunting uneasiness emanating from the persistent dream, he felt genuinely refreshed and renewed, in mind and spirit if not in body. Well, to be fair, his aging body was getting a tune-up and overhaul. He ate and drank less, with local fruit and fish making up most of his diet and he was leaner and lighter than he'd been in per-haps thirty or forty years. So now that he was so firmly and comfortably settled into his routine, he wondered why the woman, his wife Fumie, had phoned him and so urgently requested that he meet with her, granted, here on his island.

Only his current state of calm and the serenity of his emptied and well-rested mind prevented him from immedi-ately worrying about a list of possible worst case scenarios – disease, desertion, natural or financial disaster – you prob-ably know the list.

*   *   *

"What is Paradise anyway?" the Old Man once asked Ichiro when the boy was about thirteen.

"I dunno – something like Heaven maybe, or the Garden of Eden."

"Well, you have to die to get into Heaven, and all the people were kicked out of the Garden of Eden."

The boy pondered this for a moment.

"Well, maybe a place with a great beach, great weather, lots of flowers..."

"OK, now you're getting somewhere. Actually, 'Paradise' is a Persian word which means 'a walled garden'. True, the garden is fragrant with the smell of flowers and elegant with beautiful trees and stuff...but it's a walled garden and there's no way out. Paradise is peaceful and beautiful alright...but there's no escape."

"Huh...how about that."

The Old Man now knew that if his particular Paradise, walled in by the planet's most vast and enormous ocean, could in any way be compared to the Garden of Eden, then the serpent, who perhaps had been hiding silently in the grass all the while, was about to come out into the open to invade the privacy and serenity in which the Old Man had taken refuge.

The Old Man knew also that sometimes the serpent is a long dormant secret lying deep within, like that snake in the garden, hidden by the tall grass and luring one into a false sense of safety and well-being. As the Old Man had more than one long dormant secret, he had trouble focusing on which one, if any, could be connected to the increasingly ominous mood that had begun to overtake him ever since his wife had phoned him and told him she would soon be flying out to meet with him, before their agreed upon one-year separation was up.

The Old Man was spending many of his write-nothing/do-nothing hours in one of the few activities which require one to do nothing – meditation. And through his practice of meditation he had cultivated an equally do-nothing problem solving technique – dreaming. So he promised himself he would program a dream about old deep dark secrets and try to figure out how some powerful action from the long forgotten past might now be playing out its role as a catalyst for some equally powerful action in the future.

But soon enough his gloomy and foreboding mood was brightened by a humorous thought – *how much worry about the future can a man approaching his seventies have?*

*   *   *

The plane trip from Tokyo to Honolulu was 6 1/2 hours. That gave Fumie plenty of time to think about how best to break the news to the Old Man. And if that wasn't long enough, there was still the two-hour wait at the airport for the fifty minute flight to the Big Island.

The plain facts of the matter were these: she'd been to a big international comix convention in San Francisco back in April. The Old Man had been away nearly four months at the time. Although she told herself she didn't need a man in her life for sex or support – in fact, in the year leading up to his departure she and the Old Man had, albeit remaining on cordial terms, moved into separate bedrooms and had sex only three or four times a month – she didn't figure on the overwhelming sexual magnetism generated by her meeting with Max. Max was "Max Powers," the American under-ground comix artist who those in the trade were calling "the new S. Clay Wilson."

Like Wilson, who although less widely known in his time (the late 1960's and early '70's) than R. Crumb or Gilbert Shelton, was still a major player in the *Zap Comix* and Rip Off Press revolution of comix art in America, Max Powers also produced large acrylic-on-canvas paintings of certain panels of his comix epics and was fast becoming a serious force in the galleries as well as among the comic book shops, magazine stores and book sellers of Europe, the United States and Canada. So there was a buzz around him, the local guy, as there was about her, the visiting top gun (or airbrush) from Japan.

Perhaps when you have that much buzz in the air it's no surprise to find that the birds and the bees have been buzzing-ly busy, both day and night. The two talents were interviewed together, filmed together, photographed together and wined & dined together. He continually acknowledged his debt to Japanese manga art in general and to *Chibi Hanako-chan* in par-ticular. She continually acknowledged her debt to Western influences like *Zap Comix* and Rip Off Press, *Heavy Metal* Magazine, Art Spiegelman, and of course Max Powers.

So the powerful attraction between them became unde-niable and since they were so often in such close proximity during the daylight hours, it was quite human and only nat-ural that they should also cling to each other, like the proverbial iron filings to the iconographic horseshoe mag-net, during the night.

The consequential fact now, of course, was that she was carrying Max Powers' baby – or at this stage, the fetus which would become Max Powers' baby.

*   *   *

One fine, bright, cold, clear and sunny Tokyo winter day the red couch and everything the Old Man and the boy Ichiro had set up around it was gone...entirely absent. The beach was as clean as a freshly scrubbed baby's butt. They hadn't been to this particular beach for three or four weeks due to a combination of bad weather, a trip to an *onsen* hot spring resort in the mountains of Gunma Prefecture and a number of daily distractions – colds, school projects, holiday shopping.

Of course it must have been one or more of the homeless men whose blue plastic tarp covered shelters lined the river bank. In fact nearly every public park and river bank in Greater Tokyo sported scores of these *ao manshon* – "blue mansions" – as they were sarcastically called. Some were disheveled, dirty, disorderly and disgusting, while others were models of neatness and ingenuity. The latter often featured clotheslines, neatly raked walkways, welcome mats, a bicycle in good repair, all signs that the inhabitant had once been a respectable member of Japanese society, perhaps a middle manager whose company restructured and laid him off. Maybe shame – the blow to his masculine pride – had driven him out of his home, or maybe his impatient and disillusioned wife had kicked him out.

The more raggedy hovels were those of the hopelessly alcoholic or the mentally unstable or deficient. For them, a place to sleep out of the rain sufficed – indeed most bridges spanning the rivers of Tokyo supported populations who somehow managed to shut out the noise of never-ending floods of traffic and actually sleep a few hours every night. For them, neatness or cleanliness was of little or indeed no concern.

One common activity among the homeless was the collecting of cans. Unlike the West, where refundable beer and pop cans and bottles have some significant, if minimal, value – 5 or 10 cents per – in Japan they are practically, but not quite entirely worthless. The cans at least can be sold in bulk to scrap metal dealers, and every morning battalions of homeless men on one-speed *mama-chari*'s – the ubiquitous housewife shopping bicycles – often modified with an extended carrying rack over the rear fender, scour the neighborhood trash bins picking out the cans.

They then load them into huge, plastic-fiber burlapesque bags, the sheer weight and breadth of the loads mind-boggling to the casual observer, and by the noon hour return to their shanties to begin the arduous task of can smashing - , flattening every can and reducing the mass so that their precarious weekly trip to the scrap metal dealer will yield enough cash for their supply of food, or *sake* or whatever else might be deemed necessary to carry on for a few more days.

The Old Man felt no negative emotion over the disappearance of the red sofa, the two plastic coolers, the baseballs, the broom...in fact he admired the thoroughness of the operation...not a single sign left to suggest that anything as absurd as a red upholstered foam rubber Chesterfield had ever sat saucily as a tart on a barstool on a flotsam littered Kawasaki river beach.

The boy, Ichiro, shrugged and began searching the backwater for baseballs, but for some reason they were, if not totally absent, certainly in abnormally short supply on this particular day. Instead, there were scores of greenish-yellow tennis balls.

*   *   *

"Green Day"...or "Showa Day?" That was the manga mantra that first got Fumie Akahoshi in shit with the Right-wingers.

The manga story begins with Chibi Hanako-chan, in a pose reminiscent of the Silver Surfer in contemplative mode, observing a demonstration in front of the Japan Railway's Ueno Station in northeastern Tokyo. The crowds are protesting the ultra-conservative government's decision to change "Green Day" (*midori no hi*), the April 29th national holiday, the beginning of five national holidays strung together on a hit or miss basis with a Saturday or Sunday or "in between day" to make the annual springtime holiday known as "Golden Week," into "Showa Day."

The change presented an interesting dilemma. The holiday followed a rather recent – in terms of Japanese history certainly – tradition; that of celebrating the past and current Emperors' birthdays as national holidays, and except for the current, to disguise those holidays as something else. February 11th, for example, is celebrated as *kenkoku kinenbi* or National Foundation Day, and in reality celebrates the birth of Jimmu, the quasi-mythological first Emperor (660 BC) who, according legend is descended from the Sun Goddess Amaterasu.

November 3rd, the national holiday known as *bunka no hi* or Culture Day, is the birthday of the Meiji Emperor, Mutsuhito (1867-1912). December 23rd is undeceptively celebrated as *tenno no tanjoubi* or Emperor's Birthday and is indeed the day that the reigning Heisei Emperor, Akihito was born. Tellingly, August 31st, the birthday of the Taisho Emperor, Yoshihito (1912-1926), who was considered mentally deficient, is conveniently ignored and no holiday is observed.

As for Hirohito (1926-1989), posthumously known as the Showa (meaning "Bright Peace" or even "Enlightened Peace") Emperor, his April 29th birthday came to be called "Green Day" after his Imperial Majesty's alleged love of nature...(green, get it?). So in some ways, the change had the advantage of overthrowing a rather hypocritical euphemism and calling a spade a spade and a Showa a Showa. But then again, given the history of the era, especially the notorious '30's and '40's, the change was an hypocrisy itself, and perhaps one of far greater magnitude.

Anyway, in her manga story, after pondering the knotty and thorny question in regal solitude from the top of the Tokyo Tower, Chibi Hanako-chan, rather than joining the protesting demonstrators down below in railing against a *fait accompli*, through a network of highly paid spies within the Imperial Household Agency, backed up by her own steadily growing psychic powers, begins to accumulate a storehouse of information on all the comings and goings of the various members of the Imperial Family.

But, except for a rather oblique sequence – which makes a short nod or bow to the inherent nature of Japanese social tradition of inference over in-your-face embarrassing facts – alluding to the psychological anguish inflicted on the Crown Princess by the Imperial Household Agency, causing her to break out in a debilitating affliction of shingles (a particularly pernicious type of herpes viral infection), Fumie Akahoshi's popular character Chibi Hanako-chan pretty much left the Imperial Family alone.

For a while at least. But later, after the Old Man, Chibi Hanako-chan made a wrong move, Fumie Akahoshi wrote the wrong story and became, Salman Rushdie-like, marked. A *fatwah* was issued on behalf of his Majesty by the most zealous Right-wing generalissimos and all over the land of the gods Right-wingers were hallucinating themselves as the Emperor's hit men, modern ninjas or privateers, sporting sheets of Korean amphetamines and letters of marque granting them Imperial leave to murder and rape...and not necessarily in that order.

$*$ $*$ $*$

Max Powers' most notorious and lucrative creation was *Reborn* to *Raize Hell*, a serial comix story in which Jesus Christ finally returns to the earthly plane as "Jesus Christ, Robo-biker," a teenage cyborg, a 21st Century Centaur, part man (or boy), part god (or God), part Harley Davidson motorcycle. He has the power to turn water into wine, which serves him in good stead when his obviously doctored fake ID causes bartenders to refuse to serve him. He can also ride (if, indeed, that is the appropriate verb) on water, although his habit of leaking crankcase oil and axle grease on the surface of various rivers, lakes and oceans has prompted a number of environmental groups to take a wide assortment of legal and social actions against him, everything from law suits to public demonstrations, complete with sign-carrying, slogan chanting, noxious-liquid-throwing mobs of his young contemporaries protesting his arrogance and lack of concern for ecology.

His response: "In my Father's house are many mansions," went right over the heads, linguistically speaking, of these would-be ecologists who were completely unaware of the root meaning of the word under whose green, white and blue banner they so vociferously gathered. And just as the theocratic forces of Japan's Imperial Household Agency would one day focus their hostile eyes on Fumie Akahoshi's *Chibi Hanako-chan*, so were the theocratic armies of the American Fundamentalist Right, allied in uneasy partnership with the Vatican and conservative American Catholics, marshalling their considerable political influence and terrorist capabilities on Max Powers and his comix creation, Jesus Christ, Robo-biker.

What particularly angered the Catholic faction was the Origin of Jesus Christ, Robo-biker. Young Max was occasionally able to pick up CBC radio broadcasts from Canada, if his parents, Morning Glory and Max Roach were living far enough north up the California coast. The item he picked up which inspired his controversial creation was CBC's coverage of the ill-starred Papal visit to the remote Indian village of Fort Simpson, Northwest Territories. Bad weather – notably dense fog shrouding the village's tiny runway – prevented the Pope's plane from landing, but, in the hope perhaps of Divine Intervention, the pilot made one lazy circle after another above the airstrip. Meanwhile, back on the muskeg, the CBC reporter on the scene was at a loss for something to report. He took to describing the minimal infrastructure of Fort Simpson and interviewing, in their mud-spattered booths strewn here and there around the area, the vendors of Official Papal Souvenirs. The information that *Robo Cop* was playing at the village movie theatre coupled with the startling revelation that Skull & Cross-bone Pirate flags and black Harley Davidson T-shirts were the best-selling Papal souvenirs, provided in Max Powers' fertile young brain, the logical genesis of his sacred centaurial comix cyborg...and thus was created "Jesus Christ, Robo-biker – Reborn to Raize Hell!"

The Old Man was a fan of Max Powers and *JC/RB*, as he

was known to afficianados. He himself had received hate mail and death threats over *We're No Angels* and especially its sequel *We're No Saints*, although not that many TV fans in Japan, where the series originated, cared a fig or a fig leaf for Jewish or Christian theology or even knew that the Old Man ("Mr. My Room") was even connected with it, as the credits simply stated "Created by Luke Warmwater" (spewed from the mouth of the Christ) at the end of each program, by which time most viewers had already changed channels with their remotes. The Old Man had wisely refused all requests for interviews or TV appearances and while the hate mail and death threats did cause him a certain amount of sardonic concern, they were few and far enough between for him to generally dismiss them as the work of harmless cranks. After all – Salman Rushdie still lived.

*   *   *

Night fell on the Big Island as Fumie Akahoshi boarded her plane at Tokyo's Narita International Airport. The Old Man slept, dreaming of Chibi Hanako-chan and Jesus Christ, Robo-biker.

Better Future

Max Powers was conceived, born and raised on California Highway 1. His mother, Gloria Montenegro, was, in the 1960's, a hitch-hiking hippie chick known as Morning Glory. It was also known in the '60's that the seeds of the morning glory contained, along with alleged traces of strychnine, a form of lysergic acid, closely related chemically to the popular (among the hippies, at any rate) and powerful substance, LSD-25.

LSD-25 was the chemical catalyst that brought Max Powers' biological father and mother together one star-struck night in Big Sur, on the beach below Nacimiento Road. Unknown to either of the passionately fornicating hippies, however, were their given names. The two lovers fucking on the deserted beach were simply Dragonfly and Morning Glory.

When Max Powers (né Maximilian Montenegro) began asking Gloria about his father (he was about three years old the first time) she simply said: "Never trust a photographer." This admonishment became her stock answer through the years.

When little Max created a villain called "Dragonflyman" in his first comic book, drawn when he was about seven, Gloria sensed that he had supernatural, or at least psychic gifts, as well as prodigious artistic talent, and began calling him Max Powers. He liked the name very much and hung onto it – it appealed to him much more than Max Montenegro, or Max Dragonfly.

Max was born at a big beach party in Jenner, a surfer hangout not far up Highway 1 from Bodega Bay, legendary as the location of Alfred Hitchcock's suspense classic *The Birds*. By this time, Gloria – or should we say Morning Glory – had taken up with a surfer known as "Glamour Gary," the virtually anonymous photographer being a true one-night stand.

Glamour Gary was a favorite of photographers for surfing magazines, and if he'd had any real talent for surfing might have become famous enough to launch his own brand of surfboard, swim trunks or surfboard wax. But for all his glamorous looks, or perhaps because of them, Glamour Gary never rose much above Gremlin status in the surfer hierarchy. Since he knew he could never aspire to Kahunahood, he took his solace in surfer girls, hippie chicks, teeny boppers and valley girls...whatever came his way. For all Morning Glory knew, Dragonfly might have been one of the picture takers who helped immortalize Glamour Gary's tanned and blond image in the surfer press.

But by the time little Max's first birthday rolled around, there was no big party and no Glamour Gary, and Morning Glory was winding her tender tendrils around a chemical salesman – he didn't think the term "drug dealer" was at all appropriate – called "Eagle Eye Ernesto" in his cozy little seaside hideaway in Cayucos, not far down Highway 1 from the famous Hearst Castle in San Simeon. And a few months later, she and Max moved onto the combination tuna/salmon troller "Orca" – owned by Red Oker, a yoga-practicing alcoholic commercial fisherman – just a little bit further down the Highway of Broken Dreams in Morro Bay. They moved off the boat and back onto Highway 1 when the coho season opened.

*   *   *

Fumie had begun to create, in addition to the increasingly popular *Chibi Hanako-chan*, an alternative or parallel-universe Japan called "Gomi ga Shima" – literally "Garbage Island" – inspired, or perhaps we should say provoked, by the disgusting and ubiquitous mounds, piles and strews of trash left on nearly all beautiful and otherwise natural Japanese beaches, river banks, parks, shrines and green spaces, including the national symbol, Mt. Fuji, whose application to become designated a World Heritage Site has been continuously rejected because of the embarrassingly huge amount of litter and rubbish discarded along its slopes.

Naturally, she invested Gomi ga Shima with its own shadow government, shadow underworld and shadow Imperial family. It was later, after the Old Man, when the spotlight of the Japanese ultra-nationalistic, Emperor-revering Right-wingers hit the shadows of the *Chibi Hanako-chan* manga that Fumie Akahoshi found herself out of the limelight and into the burning ring of fire.

Before all the trouble started, after the first two or three years of the *Chibi Hanako-chan* manga series, she began to draw faux-educational manga, including the wildly successful *Life Cycle of the Cicada*, which became a famous short *anime,* or animation film, often played and replayed on TV, and which generated a flurry – or even a frenzy – of production and sales of stuffed cicada toys, cicada trading cards, cicada action characters and most profitable of all, a cicada computer game – *Hideous Transformer* – in which the frightening, beetle-like cicada nymphs, upon emerging through long series of tunnels in their dark, mysterious subterranean Empire, from sudden and spontaneously opening holes in the earth, are immediately and savagely attacked by a stunning array of predatory enemies – evil, hawk-like sparrows, dark, ominous jungle crows, barbaric hordes of ravenous ants.

The harassed beetles' only desire, the one object of their hideous existence, is to find a climbable vertical surface in which to insert their scythian hooks, claws and pincers so as to find a suitable perch from which they can hang, bat-like, up-side-down and, apparently, die. But although the dead shell of the beetle remains attached, belly-up to the perch, the most elegant and existential metamorphosis – molting – has just taken place.

The ugly horned and armored insect is now just empty skin, a jim-knock-care of illusion. For one brief, almost sacred moment, the shell serves as the base for the quintessential, penultimate aesthetic moment in Nature...the dramatic, ethereal appearance of a radiant winged insect angel phosphorescently glowing in the humid summer night. Seconds, which seem like eternity, later, the inevitable and unavoidable hideous transformation begins, so much more shocking in its contrast to the preternatural and ephemeral substantiation of the luminous, seraphic moth which so achingly and briefly preceded it. And next – the horror! – the inexorable devolution to a fat, brown, stubby-winged and awkward leaf-hopper begins to unfold.

As spin-offs from *Life Cycle...* gave Fumie a potent injection of cash and a promise of incalculable royalties for some time to come, she began, not unlike a denizen of the insect queendom, to become more daring and experimental in her creations – to take ever and ever greater risks. In what was fast becoming her signature or trademark style, Fumie began to blend the fantastic with the scientific. It was a style eminently suited to Japanese manga.

Re-visioning a lesson from the Chinese monk Shan Tao-kai, re-visioned much earlier by Japanese Buddhists, Fumie mixed it in with the biological description of the life cycle of the cicada. As the Japanese Buddhists would have it, "In death, Man sheds his body, as the *semi* (cicada) sheds its skin. Each reincarnation obscures memory of the previous one which is like the shed shell of the *semi*. The cicada's shell is a symbol of the early pomp of human endeavors — the hollow show of human greatness."

Modern scientists tell us that the cicada is described as "predator foolhardy." Cicadas fly poorly, don't fight and taste great.

The perfect animal for the Japanese, thought Fumie.

Among the predators on cicadas, the naturalists say, are birds of all kinds, squirrels, dogs, cats, turtles, spiders and fish.

My cast of characters, Fumie said to herself, smiling and emitting muffled grunts behind her aristocratic cheekbones. *The "whole sick crew."*

Art Spiegelman's initial concept of genius in his award-winning and epoch-making comix *Maus*, was to make the Jews mice and the Nazis cats. The Poles, she remembered, were pigs; the Americans, dogs.

People adored mice. Minnie Mouse was fashion-trendy in Japan again and Mickey Mouse, were he a three-dimensional, breathing entity capable of signing a contract would be richer than Bill Gates...by a country mile.

So OK, the Nihonjin are cicadas, the Americans will be the spiders — their Marvel Comics superhero Spiderman was box office boffo in yet another sequel and made a Special Guest Appearance in *The Final Return of the Fly.*

The Koreans will be dogs.., she smirked, instantly ashamed of herself for her inherent Japanese prejudice against their Asian neighbors.

But no need to let that little awareness get in the way, she mused while conjuring up a scene of cannibalism in a dog-eat-dog world, the lettering in hyper-modern *katakana* – sharp black angles – and a primitive fire on a river beach and slabs of dogmeat roasting, in shadow, on spits...and the dogs faintly recalling the kitschy caricatures of the pool hall, the French poodle, the beagle, the bulldog, the Great Dane....

By the same token, the Chinese will be cats.

But wait – maybe the cicadas won't be the Japanese after all.

She recalled one of those classified ads that she'd glanced over so many times in the Old Man's Monday *Japan Times*:

> CHEERFUL *Filipina wanted. Live and Filipina club* SOCIETTE *wants part-time Hostesses. Filipina only (marriage visa or permanent visa a must). High Class nightclub in Ueno. 7p.m.-1a.m. Transportation available. Room available. Salary ¥10,000~/day. Please call soon!*

"Room available". "Predator foolhardy". The cicadas will be Filipinas, the Japanese... "birds of all kinds." With this tactic she could portray against stereotype – the homogenous Japanese all birds, yes, but "birds of all kinds" preying on the "predator foolhardy" Filipinas. The possibilities were myriad and legion.

She started out by skewering corrupt and crooked politicians. One scandal followed quickly on the heels of another with alarming regularity. Faction leaders taking bribes from professional associations, fake e-mails sent to embarrass novice legislators and other dirty tricks, Cabinet Ministers pressuring and censoring the Press. But this soon proved to be too easy, and what is too easy eventually becomes too boring.

The general Japanese population was drawn as sparrows, who usually preferred other fare, and would prey on cicadas only when times were tough. The Prime Minister was a preening peacock, often drawn just emerging from a unisex beauty parlor with his head feathers just permed. Other politicians were pigeons, starlings and shrikes, who made up the ruling party and were often seen in cahoots with jungle crows, who were the *yakuza* – the gangsters. Minority parties' politicians were seagulls, wagtails, wild ducks or cormorants, depending as much on their personalities as their place on the political spectrum. A beautiful actress might be a *mejiro* or Japanese white-eye; a *yakuza* gang boss a marsh harrier or a circling black kite.

*   *   *

Max Powers, like William Shakespeare, stole good plots from wherever he could find them. One early success was a comix story based on the lyrics of Frederick "Toots" Hibbert's song "Sweet & Dandy" performed by his group *The Maytals* in the 1972 film starring Jimmy Cliff, *The Harder They Come*.

Using the Jamaican patois as text, Max skillfully drew the story of Etty's betrayal of her husband Johnson on their wedding night. Max actually considered the 1978 Jamaican indy film *Rockers* superior to *The Harder They Come*, being, in his speculative imagination, and despite the fact that he'd never been to Jamaica, a truer portrayal of the aspirations of the Trenchtown community in the 1960's & '70's. Years later, when all copyrights to the film expired, Max Powers moved in on it like a hungry shark.

There were, of course, precedents for this kind of thing. *Heavy Metal* Magazine had done Ginsberg's "Howl" as a comic strip story as well as various vignettes from the life and work of Bob Dylan in the 1970's. And to quote from his favorite story of an alternative world, Jorge Luis Borges' "Tlon, Uqbar, Orbis Tertius":

The concept of plagiarism does not exist: it has been established that all works are the creation of one author who is atemporal and anonymous....All men who repeat a line from Shakespeare are William Shakespeare.

Shakespeare, however, was too easy a target. He'd do *A Midsummer Night's Dream* or perhaps *The Tempest* as a retirement project.

Another Max Powers creation, *The Khagans of the Khazars*, was the one which earned him his first sizable group of dedicated fans. Inspired by his reading of Art Spiegelman's *Maus*, the Pulitzer Prize winning comix – or graphic novel – which tells the story of an Aushwitz survivor – Spiegelman's father – and by Borges' cryptic detective tale "Death and the Compass," Max Powers saw great story telling possibilities and unique comix perspectives in the history of the Jews. Indeed, a couple of left-leaning Depression era Jews, Jerry Siegel and Joe Shuster, created the very template for the American comic book hero, Superman.

But unlike Spiegelman, who drew from modern history, or Borges, who chose mystical sources like the *Kabala*, Max picked the Turkic Jewish Empire of the Khazars as his back story and produced great comix "Epix" on the centuries of warfare among the Orthodox Christian Eastern Roman Emperors of Constantinople, the Muslim Arabs, led by the

Caliph of Baghdad, and the Jewish converts, the Khazars, in their strongholds on the Don River and the Caspian Sea.

The contours inside the frames of Max Powers' comix took in the mountains of the Caucasus Range, the steppes and deserts of Western and Central Asia; the Mediterranean, Black and Caspian Seas. Max drew fantastic, surrealistic camels, horses, wild desert asses, leather-armored warriors armed with everything from spiked hammers to scimitars; lateen-sail rigged dhows, coursing the high, choppy main of a monstrous inland ocean, the Sea of the Khazars.

Never had the Jews been conceived, drawn and portrayed so – at least in the world of comics or cartoons – heroically. And as players, not victims. The Jews as 8th and 9th Century warriors, their cavalry traversing the steppes of Asia, their navy ruling the Caspian (Khazar) Sea, their rulers, the Khagans, building imperial cities – Itil, Sarkel, Samandar, Balanjar, Kiev – on the great seas and rivers of the time. Even the names of the Khagans – Bulan, Barjik, Baghatur – had a heroic ring. It was "Abraham meets Conan the Barbarian"... "Woody Allen morphs into Schwarzenegger."

It was through this benchmark series that Max developed his signature drawing styles – the rapidly changing perspective and the skillful deployment of maps. By consistently juxtaposing close-ups, zooms, wide-angles and bird's eye views, and moving from regular rectangular to curved, spiraled or circular panels, Max was able to produce a highly cinematic effect, which kept readers rapidly turning the pages...and buying more of his books. And by his passion for maps, especially contour maps, usually without reference to political borders, he was also able to hook the more serious readers who saw *The Khagans of the Khazars* as nothing less than a scholarly entrée into a fascinating, previously suppressed history.

*   *   *

Besides his reading, or maybe even the moment his interest in the subject was piqued and eventually led to his reading, was something he heard his Dad's friend Pablo Dread saying over and over to Marcus Neiman, their Jewish buddy – "De Rastamon is de rightful Jew."

His Dad, Max Roach, was his Mom's longest lasting boyfriend and the only one he ever thought of as "Dad," even though in age he was closer to being a big brother. His real name was Max Rausch, but the great number of joints he smoked produced the tarry, smelly but potent items that gave him his nickname. And especially, his habit of saving them in a film canister and adding their contents to all his freshly rolled doobies, made him synonymous with the powerful but harsh, evil-tasting numbers that his friends teased him over, but invariably smoked. So it was with a mixture of apprehension and anticipation that the Highway 1 hippies chanted: "Uh oh! Here comes Max Roach." The real Max Roach, of course, was sax-god Charlie Parker's drummer, not to mention jazz diva Abbey Lincoln's spouse.

His Max Roach was a drummer only in the 19th century sense – a traveling salesman. Max Roach made his way in the world hitch-hiking up and down California Highway 1 selling bags of weed...or pot...or grass, buds, whatever you wanted to call it. And whatever you called it, it was dynamite stuff, grown in clandestine, camouflaged plantations up in Mendocino and Humboldt counties, watched over by long-haired, tattooed young local rowdies or exotic international counter-culture soldiers-of-fortune from Australia, Canada, South Africa and Brazil.

Pablo Dread and Marcus Neiman were two of Max Roach's best customers. Morning Glory said she was attracted to Max Roach because he had the same first name as her baby boy, although Max Powers was already nine or ten by the time Max Roach and Morning Glory started shacking up.

Later, Max Powers realized that it was more likely the nickname that attracted Morning Glory – and she was no jazz fan.

The three caballeros also shared, in addition to the smelly, foul-tasting joints, a love of West Indian music, from steel-pan calypso to rock steady, ska and roots reggae. Pablo Dread was a drummer, in the real Max Roach 20th century sense, and played in a Santa Rosa based reggae cover band called *One Riddem*. Once a sufficient number of Max's roaches had been produced, re-rolled and consumed, Pablo Dread would launch into long and detailed explanations and interpretations of the Jamaican reggae lyrics of Bob Marley, Toots Hibbing, Peter Tosh and others to the delight of Marcus Neiman, and Max Roach...and the little hanger-on, Max Powers.

Indeed, it was while scouring Max Roach's old notebooks, left behind after he finally split up with Morning Glory and disappeared in the waters off Mexico, that Max Powers discovered the lyrics and the translation key to "Sweet & Dandy," which was one of his earliest published comix stories.

But as far as the Rastamon being "the Rightful Jew"...

Pablo's theory was that Haile Selassie, the Emperor of Ethiopia, and regarded as a diety – Ras Tafari – by the dreadlocked sect of Jamaicans known as Rastafarians, was a direct descendant of King Solomon and the Queen of Sheba, Sheba being Ethiopia. Most Jews, Pablo firmly believed, were not even descendants of the Jews of Solomon's empire, but rather, scions of the much later Khazar empire. Today's Jews, he asserted, were for the most part, not Semites at all, but

Central Asian Turks. And the Ethiopians and their exiled Jamaican cousins the Rastafarians, were "the rightful Jews."

Wow – thought Max Powers as he dug deeper into Max Roach's recorded memories... the groundwork for a sequel to his original Jamaica-based comix. *Opening frame – Haile Selassie's private Jumbo Jet motionless on the tarmac at Kingston – the Emperor, Ras Tafari himself, frozen inside, the plane surrounded by 100,000 dreadlocked, near hysterical worshippers in a collective state of rapture as they wait for God to emerge and descend the ladder. Next, back in time, a topographical map of the Holy Land, scenes of the construction of the Temple of Jerusalem, the courtship of the beautiful Sheba....*

And now, another sequel of sorts, *The Khagans of the Khazars.* If ever a ruler's formal title was made for comix, and if ever the names of cities were created for comix – nay Epix locations – Sarkal, Samarkand, Bukhara, Tashkent, Balku, Kabul... *Wow!* – thought Max Powers, his fingers itching to wrap themselves around a pen.

*   *   *

So it was in the excitement of their respective new creative ventures – Max's *The Khagans of the Khazars* and Fumie's *Gomi ga Shima* ("Garbage Island")... the world of the cicada people and their predators – that the two hot cartoonists met at the comix festival in San Francisco. And it was the excitement of their celebrity, their new creations and their dynamic introduction to one another and each other's energy that piled the pitch-wood on the fireplace of their collective imagination... and each in their own way, imagined the other to be for them, the key to a better future.

*   *   *

"I want a better future," Fumie said to the Old Man.

To the Old Man, this statement was hardly unexpected. A man heading toward 70, a woman holding off 40. What kind of future would she have with him? A housekeeper? A nurse? Indeed, the Old Man, deep into his do-nothing/write nothing year, had already retreated from their marriage, especially now that the boy, their son Ichiro, was poised to go off on his own.

The Old Man's retreat had already shown him that he too was poised to begin a new phase of his life, one in many ways not so unlike the flight of the teenager into adulthood, with all the new excitements, freedoms and... responsibilities. The only meaningful difference was that the teenager's flight was a climb into "the wild blue yonder" while the septuagenarian's would be, whether faster or slower, a descent into "the dark void" of death.

Indeed.

But he felt he was healthy enough for his age and rather than be depressed or angry or both about his being deserted – or replaced – he could just as easily be stimulated by new possibilities, essential exercise for the brain to ward off the rust and sluggishness which are the products of an uninspired mind. And while the woman, his wife Fumie Akahoshi, had been his inspiration during their nearly 20 years together, her leaving him, if the initial shock and grief didn't kill him, could actually inspire him to keep active – mentally, physically and emotionally – for perhaps another 20 or more years. At least, he felt, the odds were not so greatly stacked against him. Perhaps he could have a better future too.

"I could never really convince myself that a day like this

would never come," he heard himself saying, as if he were eavesdropping on another couple's conversation in a café.

"We often joked about it, didn't we?" she answered, trying her best to appear more light-hearted than she felt. She knew she would always hold a fondness for the Old Man. He had so often made her happy.

"We always knew there was that worm of truth hiding in the shadow of the joke."

"We gave each other a lot of good years."

"And now you're rich and famous and Ichiro is almost all grown up."

"You're not so bad off yourself."

"Depends on how long I manage to hang around. Maybe I should get alimony from you."

"Ha! Is there any wormy truth hiding in the shadows?"

"I'm glad you believe I'm joking, and I am."

"Well, I'm not when I tell you that I'm setting up a trust fund for you...to encourage long life. You won't have to worry about being old and poor. I want you to have a better future too."

*   *   *

At the Art Theater room of the plush Virgin Cinema Roppongi Hills, for all the thirty million people in greater Tokyo, the film *American Splendor*, named for the comix creation and chronicling the life of the Cleveland eccentric Harvey Pekar, its creator, failed to draw a *minyan*. Sorry Harvey, but besides a lonesome Max Powers (Fumie was appearing as a celebrity guest on a TV cooking competition show) and four couples – three hetero and one homosexual – no one else on the Kanto Plain saw fit to put out ¥1800 to sit though fifteen minutes of commercials and promotions in booming, eardrum-damaging Dolby, MC'd by a jive-talking humanoid computer voice, warning the audience not to smoke...or talk, followed by the feature film, volume appropriately pumped down. *Where is Juzo Itami when we really need him?* Max caught himself thinking. Itami's satirical *Tampopo* was Max's favorite Japanese movie.

But Max just had to see *American Splendor*. The comix had been one of Max Roach's favorites, along with S. Clay Wilson's Last Gasp Press crew – Ruby the Dyke, Captain Pissgums the Pirate, the Hog Ridin' Fools, Tree Frog Beer, Starry-eyed Stella and of course the Checkered Demon... even his evil, not to mention sick, smug and disgusting cousin, the Polka-dot Demon.

Max Roach had also been a fanatic of "The Bus," by Paul Kirchner, which appeared for several years as a subtle black & white strip in the back pages of *Heavy Metal* magazine, quite the opposite of another *H/M* comix Max Roach dug, Tamburini & Libertore's "RanXerox," rife with gory, bloody gratuitous violence and machismo rendered in screaming primary and electrified color. Of course subtlety could also be found in "RanXerox" if you knew how and where to look for it. At least Max Roach thought so.

Of course all the Highway 1 hippies loved Gilbert Shelton's *Fabulous Furry Freak Brothers* – Fat Freddie, Freewheelin' Franklin and Phineas T. – along with Fat Freddie's cat. And who could forget Shelton's answer to Siegel and Schuster's Superman – Wonder Warthog?

The oft acknowledged leader of the underground comix revolution, R. Crumb, didn't neglect to personify the animal world either, trotting out the classic neurotic, Fritz the Cat.

So Max Powers grew up with and came to also love the

underground comix his Dad, Max Roach, cherished. *Zap, Yellow Dog, Despair* and the rest beat out, in Max Powers' mind, the slicker, Euro-comix stalwart *Metal Hurlant*, which eventually morphed into *Heavy Metal* magazine and was purchased by the *National Lampoon*.

Both Maxes were fascinated by the great story telling talent and mesmerizing surrealistic rendering of the socialist realism style of Enki Bilal, whose serials, such as *The City that Didn't Exist* and the communist-era epic *The Hunting Party* appeared regularly in *Heavy Metal*, before being collected and reprinted as graphic novels. In fact, *The City that Didn't Exist* had been young Max Powers' introduction to the form.

Max Roach also collected rare independents, and until he vanished one day, presumed dead after his small sailboat was found drifting off the coast of Isla Cerralvo in the Gulf of California, was a passionate collector of *Honky Tonk Sue, the Queen of Country Swing*, starring a big breasted, larger-than-life, fast-driving, bar-hopping, Willie Nelson-loving, ass-kicking, bisexual cowgirl – she of the title – who lived in a tacky but surprisingly clean and not un-spacious double-wide in Arizona.

Max Powers had read all of these as a boy, Max Roach's what – ? son? little brother? – along with *Conan the Barbarian*, *The Silver Surfer* and *Howard the Duck*, the only three Marvel comics Max Roach allowed in the house. *Mad* was always around too – "for you, kid," as their friend Marcus Neiman used to say.

*   *   *

The big bug eyes of the cicadas made them perfect for Japanese manga. Japanese manga fans loved big-eyed, Westernized heroines – Sailor Moon and her crew being a perfect example and archetype. Fumie, however, kept Chibi Hanako-chan unabashedly Asian. She even wore her un-dyed black hair in bangs. Sexy bangs.

But in *Gomi ga Shima* she gave big, cute saucer eyes to the victims... the cicada... the Filipinas.

Looking at the cicada calmly clinging to the balcony screen in her second-floor room in Shin Maruko, Fumie could see, besides the big round eyes, the fat, curvaceous underbody ending in a soft, vulnerable, cone-shaped appendage. The antennae were short and close to the head; the wings were double-layered; like all true insects, it had six thin, jointed legs. But the most striking feature of all was how trusting it is of humans. Compare this with the mosquito, or the grasshopper, or the fly.

*   *   *

Unlike much of the Western world, where cicadas emerge only once in a generation, they are a yearly summer occurrence in Japan and avidly pursued with nets and popped into little plastic cages by youngsters all over the archipelago. When he was a boy, the Old Man remembered, he used to catch grasshoppers – he recalled only one memorable cicada phenomenon, but those insects he and his friends had mistakenly called "locusts." The grasshoppers were fed to the larger, carnivorous insects – praying mantids – which he kept in peanut butter jars with holes punched in the metal covers. Or perhaps they were preying mantids. He could never remember which.

The Old Man had once had a conversation with Max Roach long before Max's "son" came along to take away the Old Man's wife, Fumie Akahoshi. Strangely – or perhaps predictably – the conversation was about cartoons...and cartoonists. It was in a Generation X-type coffee shop in Seattle. There was a comix convention in town and Max Roach was one of thousands of enthusiasts in attendance. The Old Man, however, was not. He was simply having his habitual Café Americano in his habitual neighborhood café.

All that the Old Man remembered of their brief chat, but for some reason remembered very clearly, were Max Roach's description of his three favorite single frame cartoons. Max Roach's third favorite cartoon came from the notoriously gross and politically incorrect men's mag, *Hustler*. The cartoon was based on famous brands of peanut products popular in America at the time – indeed beyond popular, almost mandatory – peanut butter, peanut brittle, beer nuts. In those days, the top-hatted, monocled and cane-carrying Mr. Peanut roamed the downtown streets and shopping areas of American cities, big or small, on behalf of Planters Peanuts products, and TV sets incessantly intoned the commercial mantra "won't stick to the roof of your mouth" for Skippy Peanut Butter.

So in the typical crudely drawn cartoon style preferred by *Hustler*, a naked woman kneels in front of Mr. Peanut. A few random globs of smoothy peanut butter dot the otherwise bare room. Mr. Peanut's turgid peanis...well, we'll let you guess. His eyes are distinctively patrician and disinterested. The caption, obviously spoken by the kneeling woman:

"Your come sticks to the roof of my mouth."

Max Roach's second favorite cartoon was one from the famous *Far Side* by the politically acceptable Gary Larson. In this black & white syndicated newspaper panel an old English castle is prominent in the near background. The king stands on the battlements flanked by two noble knights, all three properly armed, armored and helmeted. In the foreground, a long, winding road leads up a moderately steep hill towards the castle. On the road, ascending, is a troop of barbarians, with animal skin robes and horned helmets. Each warrior carries an attaché case in his right hand. "Egad," the caption reads, spoken by the king to his retainers:

"Vikings... and they mean business."

Max Roach's #1 most favorite cartoon was another syndicated newspaper panel – *Bizarro* – by not nearly as famous, perhaps less politically correct Pisaro.

This frame is set in the middle of a desert (the ultimate labyrinth, in the mind of Jorge Luis Borges), desolate, one or two lonely cacti. Center stage, a man standing in front of a small boulder in an otherwise barren landscape. The man, dressed in cowboy fashion, has his hands bound behind his back and he looks over his shoulder back at the rock with a quizzical expression. Around the rock are a few black-hatted cowboys...obviously bad guys... and their horses. Perhaps there's a bag of money lying around. Perhaps not. Positioned across the rock is an 8' long, 6"x12" plank.

The focus of the frame, however, is on the leader of this gang of outlaws. He is placed just off to the right and a little behind the boulder and the plank. His expression is one of puzzled bewilderment. He has a wooden leg, a parrot on one shoulder, a patch on one eye, a striped bandana on his head in lieu of a cowboy hat and a turned down high leather boot on his one foot. He is armed with a cap & ball pistol and a cutlass. The caption is his:

"Hmmm, we always did it this way at my old job and it worked real well."

Prosperity

In their courtship days in Seattle, the Old Man remembered once telling Fumie "in order to understand American culture, ya gotta understand peanut butter." In truth, he didn't know why that random memory was coming to him now, now that he and Fumie were discussing their impending divorce. He had the vague and fleeting thought that it might somehow be connected to the recurring dream he'd been having, the one in which he was being approached by a shadowy older son.

The Old Man knew that no one can monopolize the Muse, and while he first thought of her as a kind of magician's beautiful assistant, in the days when he was still a photographer and she his occasional model, frequent translator and consistent interpreter of Japanese culture, his creative Muse she had gradually turned out to be. He owed his Biblical revisions in creating *We're No Angels* for the Japanese TV audience in no small measure to her. And since he knew that no one can monopolize the Muse he had fairly long ago accepted that his time with her was likely to be impermanent. Neither Japanese marriage certificates nor wedding ceremonies mention any phrase equivalent to "Until death do us part."

In fact, both getting married and getting divorced were relatively simple procedures in Japan. One simply filled out a form at the local ward, town or city office and registered the event. Divorce, if not contested, was even simpler than marriage. Ridiculously simple...and fast. And the Old Man was not considering refusing Fumie's request.

For one thing, he had some potentially serious health issues to deal with, mentally, physically, psychically and emotionally, and he didn't feel like boring the hell out of everyone around him or sabotaging his own mind/body equilibrium that would bring him through any crisis alive, and "with all his faculties intact," at least as far a person of his age could expect. Intellectually, and indeed that was the realm in which he found himself to be increasingly functioning, he could see no advantage in acrimony, and emotionally – well, his very years, combined with his current self-imposed isolation and inactivity had given him a detachment which is one of the mixed blessings of aging.

He didn't feel like crying yet. He wondered if...or when...Fumie would cry.

*   *   *

Some years later, when he was 84 years old, he wrote his famous novel *The 124 Year Old Man*. It was perhaps at the very moment of this climax to his love affair and marriage with Fumie that he gave in to a long-held, oft-cherished secret desire, one for a long time fogged over by self-doubt; to write a quality work of serious literary fiction and to leave behind the only worthwhile thing a person can leave behind...a legacy...or more precisely, a good name.

*   *   *

Max Powers also had some famous literary works ahead of him and indeed, despite the fact that his attackers often accused him of things like "ripping off Rip Off Press", his response to the scholars and critics was to quote Borges from "Tlon, Uqbar, Orbis Tertius" and to hacks and reviewers, Abbey Hoffman's *Steal this Book*.

His move to Tokyo with Fumie Akahoshi was a catalyst precipitating an explosion.

A T-shirt he saw a woman wearing on a subway – *The King of Tongue Lashing* – was lifted directly to the title of a wickedly venal, obscene, perverse and hilarious 12 page color comix story in *Heavy Metal* magazine. The tragic death of a small boy in a revolving door at a luxurious Roppongi Hills condominium tower gave birth to the sardonically saccharine/scathingly activist series in a popular Tokyo-based English language magazine, "Attack of the Killer Doors," which initiated a run of lawsuits and a straight-to-video movie about a sleazy lawyer who finally straightens-up-and-flies-right while suing high-flying, high-tech, high-rolling, high-rise construction companies back to earth on behalf of suitable pitiable child victims of modern architecture and their angry and often schizophrenic bereaved parents. Profits from the movie paid the lawyers' fees.

On a more philosophical level he did another magazine series called "My Inscrutable Neighbor Tanaka-san" in which the incredible degree of scrutiny under which the Japanese people survives is exposed as a rallying cry to the small population of Japanese dissidents and a wake-up call to Japan-based ex-patriates to examine their own takes and spins on stereotyping and xenophobia. After a few installments, the series created enough of an international buzz that his agent, Wiley Moon, was able to sell an episode to the *New Yorker*, thus bringing Max Powers into the rarified comix air breathed by the likes of Art Spiegelman and Robert Crumb.

The *New Yorker* episode followed one of Max Powers' regular writing habits, looking up the derivation of key words and tracing them back to their original meaning in their original language. He traced the adjective "inscrutable" (not easily understood; obscure; unfathomable; enigmatic) from the noun "scrutiny" back to the Latin verb "*scrutari*" meaning to search – originally "to sort rubbish" from the Latin noun "*scruta*" meaning rubbish.

This particular story follows the early morning route of a typical Japanese neighborhood "garbage cop", usually an elderly man who checks to see whether anyone is putting out their garbage too early, not sorting it into the proper containers and the like. When the garbage cop rings the doorbell of the narrator – the one foreigner in the neighborhood – to complain that he's put out his garbage ahead of the official garbage-putting-out time – the narrator seeks the help of his inscrutable neighbor Tanaka-san, which opens a very unexpected can of worms.

Another of Max Powers' penchants was seeing synchronicities and interpreting them as examples of destiny or fate. The fact that Fumie Akahoshi's *Gomi ga shima* (Garbage Island) and *My Inscrutable Neighbor Tanaka-san* turned trash into cash for both of the newlyweds could hardly escape Max's notice.

It all reminded Fumie of her ecstatic delight in rummaging through files and piles of old underground comix from the 1960's, '70's and '80's during her stay in San Francisco for the Comix Convention. R.L. Grabb's *Little Greta Garbage* immediately grabbed her attention vis à vis *Gomi ga shima* and led her to raiding all the Bay area university libraries to make copies of original *Little Orphan Annie*, the famous Sunday newspaper comic strip.

Dennis Cramer's fantasy/adventure *Mara of the Celts* was, Fumie thought, an interesting take on Japanese manga. The Celtix heroines were romantically drawn, with the big eyes favored by Japanese artists, but their sexuality was definitely womanly, not childish. They had big tits, but, unlike classic Corben, they weren't disturbingly big. She could see their influence on Max Powers' warrior women in *The Khagans of the Khazars*.

Both were similar to Trina Robbins' romantically drawn heroines in *Near Myths* – Robbins eschewed big eyes altogether – but not nearly so over-the-top as the scantily costumed, big eyes/big tits humanoid she-wolves of See Wolf's *The Magical Nymphimi*.

She also found one-offs like the old Rip Off standby nebbish Philbert Desenex in *Phigments* or one of Max Powers' personal sacred relics, *The Renegade*.

She found Brice Bolinger's 1990's series *Stranger in a Strange Land Comix; True Tales of an aging hippie lost somewhere in the Bible Belt*, a pure Rip Off rip-off of Robert Heinlein's SF classic of the same name, much beloved by the '60's hippies for coining the verb and the concept *to grok*, meaning to completely, instantly and psychically understand something another person is thinking. Acid dropping hippies were grokking – or trying to – all the time, and the concept eventually found its way, with unexpected consequences, into the psychic powers developed by Chibi Hanako-chan.

Later, she'd be glad that she'd bought a set of underground jewels in a vintage comix shop – which she took along to Hawaii to help cheer up the Old Man – from the heyday of S. Clay Wilson, R. Crumb and Gilbert Shelton: *Zap, Bijou, Big Ass, Creem* and *Despair*.

*   *   *

Together in Tokyo, while the Old Man continued to write nothing/do nothing in Hawaii – except perhaps for reading the old comix – Fumie Akahoshi and Max Powers scoured the chaotic, crowded streets for ideas. And once again the inscrutable T-shirt provided the inspiration. This was in a back alley in a run-down working-class neighborhood in Ota Ward. An *ojiisan*, an old man, mounted an old, dusty, beaten up motor-scooter – firing it up proved it to be out of tune as well – and haltingly propelled it onto a shopping street. His movements were slow enough so they could both read the entire message encoded in cracked and faded yellow paint on a once red, washed-out background:

RACING FUEL
I continue to walk
on the wonderful
World Road

Thus was born their first collaboration, *Old Coot on an Old Scoot Funnies.*

*   *   *

Fumie Akahoshi and Max Powers both knew, while they disported themselves with appropriately inappropriate abandon in Tokyo, that Fumie was carrying Max's baby and that all this would have to be explained to the boy, Ichiro, her and the Old Man's son – now a teenage high-school student – who was spending summer vacation with his maternal grandparents in their big old house in central Japan, while Fumie got on with her burgeoning career and the Old Man indulged in his nothing/ nothing retreat in Hawaii. The Old Man and the boy's grandparents were not so far apart in age.

But as long as Ichiro was out of sight for the nonce, he could also be left safely out of mind. And there were plenty of other less personal if no less significant issues to concern them. Fumie and Max were sitting in a Starbucks café in Tokyo, in Nihonbashi, not far from the Ginza. There were so many Starbucks in Tokyo now one would think they were a Japanese chain, like Yoshinoya or Ito Yokado. Max was checking out the English-language press.

Two Letters to the Editors (page 4) debated the hooliganism of Chinese soccer fans against the visiting Japanese at the recently played Asian Cup. The pro-Japanese letter (name & prefecture withheld) concluded: *We Japanese can't build a productive relationship with people like that.*

The pro-Chinese letter (name & prefecture given) ended as follows: *Since the Japanese government – due to pressure from Right-wing politicians – is dead set against showing sincere contrition at the highest levels, Japan can expect this sort of behavior to continue for many years to come.*

The contrition, as Max surmised and Fumie confirmed, was over Japan's war-time atrocities, especially the infamous Mengele-esque Manchurian medical experiments, the Nanking massacre and the use of Asian women – euphemistically designated "comfort women" – as sex-slaves for the Japanese Imperial forces.

Moving on to News of the World (page 7) a picture (Reuters photo) caught Max's eye, along with its lead: *Donald Duck gets star on Hollywood Walk of Fame.* The photo showed a costumed Donald Duck character pointing to his star in the sidewalk during an apparently serious ceremony. "Did you know that Donald Duck comics and cartoons were once banned in Finland?" Max asked.

"No, really? Why?"

"Because he doesn't wear pants."

There were also News Briefs on the same page and Fumie was attracted to *Blue-eyed stripeless tiger born in Spain* and she read it out to Max ...*such tigers are sometimes born in the wild, but it is almost impossible for them to survive for long as their strange coloring causes them to be rejected or even attacked by other tigers.*

"The nail that sticks up gets hammered down...big time," Max offered.

"You got that right," Fumie replied.

Max then noticed another News Brief, AP dateline, Manila: *Four held for killing, eating family member.*

"And these, I take it, were not tigers."

"Nope," said Max.

And all this was the mainstream press.

*   *   *

Japan provided the stimulus, the catalyst, the impetus for a two year long string of manga and comix triumphs for Maxx Powers and Fumié Akahoshi, both as individuals and as collaborators. (When her new boyfriend asked her how to become instantly popular as an artist in Tokyo she immediately replied "Add another 'X' to your name." So Max became Maxx and she added the accent acute over the "e" to slightly Westernize and at the same time accent the proper pronunciation of her name.) Maxx ripped off the clearly purloined banner and slogan of a used book store he visited near a university campus in western Kanagawa Prefecture: "Starbooks – you are what you read" – to create a critically acclaimed series by the same name, which didn't make him a fortune, but raised the credibility of the publisher – *Heavy Metal* Magazine – in the estimations of the academic and intellectual communities which led to Maxx getting a multi-series + book contract with the mag and an affiliated major book publisher.

The series begins with a Harvey Pekar-like bookshop owner crackle-barreling homespun humor about books and duchying homegrown weed around the 4'x8' pool table in the back of his shop, while his Addams-family cos-play Japanese wife kibbutzes with her Mad mix of traditional Japanese and modern anarcho-punk perspectives. The episode featuring Anaïs Nin's erotic tale "The Veiled Woman" spawned a flurry of articles among the intellectual periodicals community, with revisionist *feuilletons* on feminism, men's movements and political correctness being the order of the day. The next episode, however, *Moby Dick*, shoulder-held rocket launched all those pretensions with its mondo bizarro fable involving genital herpes and a candidate for the baseball Hall of Fame.

Fumié translated the series *Pot Boilers* which then found its way into the best-selling manga *Business Jump*, which didn't do a hoot for the manga's IQ ratings, but in terms of ¥en, more than doubled Maxx's fees for the entire rest of the year-long series. The scene of Popeye raping Temple Drake with a corncob from Faulkner's *Sanctuary* played well to Japanese manga fans, rape fantasy and perverse porn being essential elements in nearly all "men's" manga.

But the classic episode for many was the one in which an

underachieving university student reads J.D. Salinger's *Nine Stories* and becomes "The Laughing Man," studying the languages of a variety of woodland and domestic animals, keeping a large and loyal wolf for a pet, occasionally wearing a red poppy-petal mask.

Fumié, meanwhile, was also becoming a media darling for her acceptance as an important artist by America. Even the most fragmented connection with "other" countries or "foreigners" was considered newsworthy internationalism in homogeneous, xenophobic, neo-nationalistic Japan. And on the spiked or platformed heels of media attention in Japan, comes the *terebi tarento*, the "TV Talent", a sort of talking upper body for absurd panels or asinine game shows featuring other *tarentos* mouthing meaningless platitudes, while behind them, but not far in the background, sexily dressed wannabe *tarentos* smile and enthusiastically nod their heads after every banal remark...a silent charade of the ubiquitous "*Hai!*"

Fumié found herself shrieking in disbelief when a pitiably homely, pockmarked, misfit young loser is transformed for the studio audience into a sexy-cute *fashionista* by the makeover miracle of cosmetic surgery & esthetics, make-up artists, hair & fingernail stylists, clothing designers and despicable yet irresistible scorning ex-boyfriends for only ¥3,800,000, or roughly $35,000. As a world-famous cartoonist, she gets to sit on the "panel" with a few other shifty-eyed celebrities and collect a fee that could buy the poor girl's transformation several times over.

The next day she's competing against an aging boy-toy pop singer on a cooking competition. It's her Nagoya *Kochin Oyako-don* chicken and egg stew over rice versus his Nagasaki *Champon* pork and seafood noodle soup. And on the weekend it's watching the video-taped travelogue of yet another pop star who visited the exotic coast of Madagascar to hunt for the living fossil fish coelacanth and to treat the native fishermen & fishwives to home-made coelacanth sashimi. Here the panel tries to guess answers to trivia questions generated by his fascinating, 5-day adventure in a foreign land.

But when she wasn't *tarento*-ing around Tokyo TV, Fumié Akahoshi was working with Maxx Powers on *Old Coot on an Old Scoot* and its disheveled, befuddled *ojiisan* hero Goto-san. Goto-san, published in Japanese in the quarterly *Big Comic* and in English in the monthly *Japanzine* became not only a billboard for bad English T-shirts — which changed with every new strip — but also an *anime* character on a Sunday evening TV animation program, complete with a product line of bad English T-shirts, including cuties for kids and twenty-something female *fashionistas* and lewdies for teens; both cute stuffed and tough action characters, and of course, key ring and cell-phone holder ornaments.

Some of Goto-san's most popular T-shirts, after *RACING FUEL* of course, were:

Black Butterfry

———

To Be Hang Ten,
is to
Be Cool

———

Drink and Smell

———

Feminine Surf
is my middle
name

———

Keep Your Eyes

————

The Pure Atmosphere
which is fantastic
though it is deep

————

Maxx's own personal favorite was:

Live as a Friend
with Fruit.

All Goto-san's T-shirts carried slogans Maxx actually saw on the Tokyo transit system or on the streets.

The names in the Old Coot's scoots would subtly change in one panel per episode: Yamaha Vino would become Wino; Honda, Fonda and so on.

Goto-san occasionally made guest appearances in *Gomi ga Shima*, usually when his visit to the funny animal world as a human 'toon could be linked with the latest scandal story in the Japanese press. **Another Nuclear Plant Fatality**, for example, found the Old Coot with a passenger on the back of his Old Scoot...it's none other than Bart Simpson – *The Simpsons* re-runs being popular on Japanese TV – recently graduated from Springfield A & M, come to run the Gomi ga Shima nuclear power plant industry as head of its Atomic Energy Commission.

Maxx's *Khagans of the Khazars* expanded its horizons and locations eastward across Central Asia, to the very borders of the Han Empire, where oriental dragon ladies, con-tributed by Fumié, enticed Maxx's Jewish-Turkic nomads in luxurious palaces and spacious desert tents, fragrant with the heady odor created by a mélange of sweat, perfume, horse-flesh, hashish, musk, old blood, incense and the remnants of imperfect digestion that the heroes carried with them from the west.

Maxx also had another cross-over success with new adventures of *Jesus Christ, Robo-biker*, the famous baseball series, in which JC/RB rides into an alternative world, "Planet of the Abes," where the Cleveland Jews of the Continental League face the Atlanta Rabbis of the Oceanic League in the Planetary Series of Baseball. It was popular on both sides of the Pacific. The baseball connection and the interest in western religions sparked, in part, by the Old Man's *We're No Angels & We're No Saints* TV sitcoms, conviced the giant *Shuueisha* manga publishers to translate "Planet of the Abes" for one of their ever popular *Jump* weekly manga magazines.

But the real maraschino cherry atop the fabulous road to riches sponge cake concocted in the new Roppongi Hills studio of the cross-cultural dynamic duo, was *Alpha Mind Control Comics*, inspired by Maxx, but almost entirely drawn and written by Fumié. In this breakthrough manga series, two stripeless, tigers, one white, the other blue, the former living on Mt. Kilimanjaro and the latter in a bamboo forest in Central China, are channeled by Chibi Hanako-chan, who uses them to K.O. cancer cells through the power of psychic visualization.

The series became fanatically popular in Japan, emerging from the underground nests of its early cult status like an endless chain of cicadas and transforming into something of an institution following a government sponsored report confirming that the rate of cancer remission among regular readers and fans was 70% higher and the incidence of new cancers 70% lower than in the general population. The metaphysical "Hundredth Monkey" Theory used to explain this phenomenon held that Japan's enormous population density – as high as 13,000 or more people per square kilometer in Tokyo for example – made it much easier than in other places for Critical Mass to occur.

The series created an economic breakthrough for Fumié as well. Convinced that her publisher was wrong by insisting that she expunge the words "Mind Control" from the title – they thought people would confuse it with "thought control" – Fumié set up her own independent imprint – "Brain Wave Press" – and by cutting out the greedy middleman became one of the wealthiest women in Japan.

*   *   *

The Old Man was hardly the wealthiest man in Hawaii, or even in his new home town, which was inhabited by more over-the-hill but financially secure aging former rock stars than you could shake an electric bass at – or in the Old Man's case, a garden hoe. The Old Man lived well enough on the various royalties he'd collected through the years by his various "artistic" endeavors. The re-run and video payments from *We're No Angels*, which became extremely popular in China, Malaysia and Singapore, more than paid the rent.

The Old Man's coffee farm and organic garden, while still in the red financially, nevertheless put tasty and healthy food and drink on the table for the Old Man and the boy, Ichiro. Ichiro, as a Japanese-American, felt more at home in Hawaii than he could ever hope to in Japan and, settling in with the Old Man after the split with Fumié, remained to become manager of the coffee farm and left the gardening to the Old Man.

With the virtual de-criminalization of *pakalolo* in Hawaii and the legalization of medical marijuana – liberally prescribed by local docs for a myriad of symptoms and syndromes, ranging from sinus headaches to terminal cancer and AIDS – a lot of the Old Man's hobby farming was devoted to cultivating and camouflaging – against raids by gangs of teenagers – a modestly sized but powerful crop of cannabis.

The years following his divorce from Fumié Akahoshi passed quickly – maybe too quickly for a man leaving his '60's and entering his '70's – but aside from the infrequent bout of sadness caused by sentimentality or nostalgia, the Old Man had little difficulty adjusting to the loss of his wife and return to bachelorhood which, after all, had been his condition for the better part of his adult life.

Ichiro's company kept him from being alone and he occasionally found female companionship, whether from the ubiquitous troupes of middle-aged female tourists, the odd younger woman – usually artistic or intellectual types – or even someone connected to show business, an arena in which he was still required or requested, once in a while, to show his face.

But his secret passion was his pursuit of literary perfection...the continuous writing, revising and re-writing of his pet project, his seemingly perpetual work-in-progress, the story he called "The 124 Year Old Man."

*   *   *

Back in Tokyo, after their initial burst of erotic and artistic energy, Fumié Akahoshi and Maxx Powers found that their respective paths were increasingly branching out in different directions. Fumié's popularity in Japan led to a string of lucrative TV commercials and endorsements for typically female products – *ume shu*, a plum flavored liqueur marketed to women, a famous brand of cold green tea sold in plastic bottles from vending machines, a line of sexy underwear by a renowned fashion designer, as well as Apple computers, a Japanese internet provider and a European cell-phone manufacturer. She drew the line at cigarette commercials, but otherwise showed little or no resistance to "selling out."

After all, Fumié had two babies to support now – Bird, her and Maxx's new son, named for Charlie Parker, and Maxx Powers himself, who had a good literary reputation and a cult following, but came nowhere near his wife in earning power. She bought a huge house in Den-en-chofu, the toniest and most expensive residential town in Tokyo and a big new condominium cum studio for Maxx in Roppongi Hills, "Tokyo's most fashionable address" according to the real estate promotions.

While the studio was one floor above the original one she shared with Maxx and still paid rent on, Fumié preferred to stay at home in Den-en-chofu and created a spacious studio and workshop of her own in her luxurious house. Maxx spent more and more time away from Japan, keeping a small apartment in San Francisco and a modest beach house in Baja California Sur, Mexico.

Although Maxx Powers was one of America's most famous comix artists, his work remained essentially "underground" and never did the sales of his works approach the numbers put up by mainstream comics like Marvel's *X-Men*, *Spiderman* and other super-hero standards. Nor did Maxx's controversial or off-beat tales spin off into blockbuster summer movies.

But Maxx Powers, like the Old Man, also had a secret goal, a pet project if you will, a study of the role of mice in

American art and pop culture.

For starters, Mickey Mouse, Walt Disney's proto-type cartoon mouse, was the richest entity in the world. Although never alive, he outlived his creator, the conservative cartoonist who gave him life. Or maybe it was the creation, Mickey, who breathed life into the creator, Walt. Many spoofs, inevitably and inexorably followed through the years. Mad Magazine did "Mickey Rodent" which examined the phenomenon of funny animals having four fingers on each hand as well as a set of white gloves. Rip Off Press did the sinister *Mickey Rat*. Art Spiegelman did *Maus*, followed by *Maus II* (*Mauschwitz*) which won him the Pulitzer Prize.

And although Maxx was in no way an anti-Semite or a Nazi, he couldn't help but agreeing with part of the 1930's German newspaper article quoted by Spiegelman as the frontispiece of his prize winning graphic novel: *"Mickey Mouse is the most miserable ideal ever revealed...the dirty and filth-covered vermin, the greatest bacteria carrier in the animal kingdom, cannot be the ideal type of animal.... Down with Mickey Mouse."*

Then there were the "copyrats" like Jerry and Mighty Mouse and in Japan, Shigeru Mizuki's evil but cowardly Ratman. And where there's mice, there's cats — Felix, Tom, Sylvester, Fritz, Spiegelman's Nazis, Mizuki's Catgirl. And in this murine cosmology, ducks were the coyotes. Donald, Daffy, Howard... "trapped in a world (t)he(y) never made."

Provocative as this project might potentially be, there was a higher, if less idealistic priority for Maxx Powers, the one and only spin-off that could possibly put him on a financial footing with his apparently erstwhile A-listed wife, Fumié Akahoshi, and that was a Game. Top Games, megabuck producers themselves now that Games were the best-selling form of media entertainment, also produced a geometric expanse of spin-offs: cards, toys and action figures; animation TV shows and movies; fan magazines; fashion items, both apparel and accessories...you name it. Eventually, even the most kick-ass character, like Chibi Hanako-chan, would become, through relentless productification & spinoffiliza-tion...Mickey Moused. But, like monsieur M/M himself, wealthy beyond words.

Beneath the sardonic mask of his alter-ego JC/RB, Maxx Powers thirsted for that kind of wealth.

*   *   *

The first two years they were together were the peak years in Fumié Akahoshi's life with Maxx Powers. Maxx, born in the Year of the Rat (or the Mouse), was consumed with nervous energy, which he exploited by a sometimes overbalanced mixture of creative bursts growing out of his self-exile in his darkened studio, lit only by a spotlight focused on his drafting table, followed by whirlwind odysseys of socialization – attending comix conventions, vis-iting literary shrines, schmoozing at art galleries, adventure touristing in tropical locations close to the sea.

So after Maxx and Fumié signed a lucrative character product contract for the use of "Goto-san" and other images from *Old Coot on an Old Scoot*, the hard-charging dynamic duo headed for one of Maxx's favorite getaways, Todos Santos, in Baja California, Mexico.

It was the first real vacation they took together since their initial typhoon of a romance, which climaxed nine months later in the tsunami of baby Bird's arrival. They now deemed Bird old enough to travel, "Old Coot" was providing the meal ticket and all signs indicated that a kickback vacation was in the cards.

Maxx leased a little 5-room casa near the beach in Todos Santos. Fumié and Bird would be able to spend hours together playing on the beach while Maxx had "free time". Then Maxx and Bird would spend hours together playing on the beach while Fumié had "free time". For the next two weeks no "work" was to be done. Perhaps the Old Man's "write nothing/do nothing" influence was still with her.

But then, after only four days, Maxx blew it all by flying up to San Jose to meet with a big-time Game producer about spinning off some of his comix characters into Games.

Maxx Powers' trip turned out to be largely a waste of time, the only result being firmly told that the rights to neither *The Khagans of the Khazars* nor *Jesus Christ Robo-biker* would be purchased by the company.

After several days of Maxx Powers completely failing to hear the truth between the empty phrases of corporate double-speak – or *tatemae* as it was called in Japan – he was finally taken to lunch at a subdued and yuppified restaurant by an extremely young product development jr. executive and informed that the market for Jewish fantasy/action heroes among the 8-10 year-old demographic, which was fantasy/action's target audience, was virtually zilch – even in Israel – and that Right-wing Christian Fundamentalist lobbies would never let anyone get away with mainstreaming *JC/RB*. Game over!

Maxx Powers left San Jose feeling frustrated, angry and depressed and in no mood to inflict his condition on Fumié and Bird. Nor did he feel like he could enjoy lounging on the beach at Todos Santos. So, neglecting to phone, e-mail or even send a post card, Maxx instead rented an RV camper van and proceeded up the coast, nursing his negativity with a mixture of George Dickle's Tennessee sour mash and hydroponically grown, medical-grade marijuana.

Foolhardily risking detection and arrest by smuggling his comfort contraband recreational substance, he decided to continue north into Canada, choosing the ferry across Juan da Fuca Strait from Port Angeles on the Olympic peninsula to Victoria on Vancouver Island as the likeliest route for avoiding a thorough-going customs inspection – ferries, after all, had to run on schedule.

Bad luck did not follow him across the border and later that night he felt that maybe his luck was changing for the better as he lay out on Long Beach on the west coast of the island, sipping from a flask of Canadian Club and toking on a huge spliff of his successfully smuggled sensemilla. It took him almost a week of self-indulgent R & R before he was ready to return to the family vacation he had so self-centeredly broken up. Fortunately, he was focused enough to e-mail Fumié from his cell phone: "Shit hit fan in San Jose. Cleaning up in Canada. See you next week. Maxx."

* * *

Well, he's not dead or in jail, Fumié reasoned, choking down her rising anger with a minimal feeling of relief. Bird's response to his father's absence was less than minimal, feeling much more comfortable at his tender age with his mother. And besides, the sparsely populated town, the nearly empty beach and the bare, spacious landscape – desert descending down from the mountains to the sea – was such a welcome contrast to the humid pressure cooker of summer in Tokyo –

the hot, heavy air and the masses of sweaty people pressing in on all sides the moment she left the air-conditioned comfort of her luxurious new home.

So she settled into a routine of temporary single-motherhood, rising early to the first light as the sun peeked out of the Gulf of California, still invisible behind La Giganta Mountains, and to the haunting, funereal chorus of the mourning doves.

Fishing, Farming, Business

While Fumié Akahoshi and her young son Bird Powers swam and played on the beach at Todos Santos, a little further up the coast, at Puerto San Carlos in Bahia Magdalena, the Silver Surfer was tying up the mooring lines of *Los Derechos del Hombre* in preparation for off-loading its catch of albacora, bonito and dorado at the fish buyer's creaky wooden dock.

The Silver Surfer was, in fact, Jorge Luis Valenzuela, the bastard son of Beatriz "Becky" Valenzuela, a repatriated Mexican-American from New York City, and a vacationing college student from somewhere in American California, who had fornicated with Becky on a beach somewhere in Baja California Sur during a Spring Vacation some 20 years past.

Although Jorge Luis had been conceived down here in Mexican California, he'd been born and raised on the Big Island of Hawaii, where his nomadic mother, always more comfortable speaking English than Spanish, decided to go and live after two missed periods in a row convinced her that she'd have better luck as a single parent in Hawaii than in a conservative Mexican small town, wedged in between the mountains, the desert, and the sea.

Despite being a New Yorker in culture and thinking, she was still Catholic enough to reject the possibility of even thinking about an abortion. Once settled in Hilo, Hawaii, she managed to get by giving Spanish lessons, which also kept her in touch with the language, and by making puka shell jewelry which she sold to gift shops and at Saturday morning farmers' markets.

After Jorge Luis, known among his schoolmates and surfing buddies as "Captain George," graduated from high school, the two of them returned to Baja, and with the money Becky had painstakingly saved, and increased with a few well-chosen investments in high-tech stocks – she was, after all, still a New Yorker at heart – bought a whitewashed casa in Todos Santos, a small cosmopolitan community well stocked with artists, writers and intellectuals.

But before the move, and the most important contributor to it, was the dramatic – or should we say traumatic – event which occurred during Jorge Luis' junior year of high school year at an inter-island surfing competition on the north shore of Oahu.

While paddling on his long board, getting in position for the next set of waves, Jorge Luis, to his horror, spotted a shark fin moving at great speed and heading his way. He managed to pull all his limbs out of the water the moment the shark struck, taking a chunk of fiberglass-coated styrofoam out of his surfboard.

Apparently disgusted by the taste and texture of the above mentioned man-made morsel, the shark turned and struck again, successfully biting off the lower right leg of a neighboring surfer who was sitting astride his board, waiting for the swells to build.

Although the victim made it to the beach, he died of blood loss before a tourniquet could be applied by the frantic officials of the competition. Jorge Luis, who in his terror was unable to produce a sound, blamed himself for not warning the other surfers of the shark. And the same terror that rendered him temporarily mute also produced a more permanent effect – it turned his hair completely white, or more accurately, a shade of gray which could quite reasonably be described as silver.

It wasn't until he and Becky had moved back to Baja and he began surfing again around Todos Santos that he picked up the nickname. And like many young surfers he was a comix fan and one of his favorites – he couldn't bring himself to read the adventures of his namesake... too many bad memories – was *Newt Quest*, a new series by Maxx Powers.

*   *   *

Newt Quest was Maxx Powers' response – although some might say rip-off – of one of his favorite comix in his own youth, Wendy & Richard Pini's *Elf Quest*, along with Czech Science Fiction writer Karel Capek's novel *War with the Newts* which he discovered much later in life.

Beginning with a single strip in *Heavy Metal* called "The Eagle & the Newt," in which a lowly newt saves his life by entering into an irony-tinged intellectual discourse with a hungry and predatory eagle, *Newt Quest* soon developed into its own comic book and quickly gained a kind of cult status, especially among male university students and other similarly aged slackers. It could, Maxx hoped, be the key, if he played his cards right and could resist letting it become too politically subversive, to his avidly sought-after goal of being the creator and financial beneficiary of a Game.

*   *   *

Chibi Hanako-chan's love interest and Watson to her Holmes, was Dorado-kun, a precocious high school student, whose name could also be read as "dolphin fish" in English, "*mahi mahi*" in Hawaiian and "*shiira*" in Japanese. "Dorado" was the Spanish name for the sleek golden pelagic predator, but had the literary advantage of being phonetically easy to transliterate into Japanese. In fact in the pages of her ever popular manga, Fumié Akahoshi used all the various spellings available to her – both the *katakan*a and *hiragana* syllabic forms as well as the alphabetically derived *romaji* – at various times to refer to her heroine's (usually) faithful companion. And she was quite expert in selecting the right lettering style to enhance the mood of any given panel.

Dorado-kun was portrayed as an 18-year-old 3rd year (Senior) student at Nakagomi High School, shy but handsome in a deceptively conventional manga style for male protagonists, with lots of sharp angles on the haircut, the eyes and the eyebrows, and the parts of the black, military-style school uniform which covered the body's joints. He occasionally, for one frame only, morphed into Archie, Reggie or Jughead, depending on the situation.

Resisting the urge to put Dorado-kun on a skateboard, Fumié gave him a souped-up BMX bicycle instead, with radically beefed-up and chromed rear-axle bolts on which a female passenger like Hanako-chan or perhaps a pleated-mini-skirt wearing high school girl could ride, standing up, with her arms encircling Dorado-kun's waist or at least with her hands resting on his shoulders. The 19th Century German cadet style stiff-collared, brass-buttoned boys' uniform and the suggestive midi-blouse, mini-skirt and knee-sox outfit of the girls, were all a cartoonist needed to emphatically illustrate the sexist double standard common – nay, endemic – in Japanese culture and society.

While Chibi Hanako-chan and Dorado-kun were essentially

social justice advocates, they both had very human as well as very typically Japanese character flaws and weaknesses. Indeed, their lack of consistent superhero characteristics – their "everyperson" human-ness – along with their in-your-face, diabolically clever and consummately cool modus operandi in regard to problem solving was what most endeared them to their Japanese readership and translated reasonably well to their English language version fans.

To reinforce a gender-inclusive appeal and thereby widen its demographic, Fumié used a technique she remembered from *Elf Quest*, which was drawn by Wendy Pini, the female co-creator. Fumié had become a fan of *Elf Quest* back in the days when she was a massage therapy student in Seattle. The technique was combining the fluid and expressive style typical of female comics artists with the more macho male artist qualities of power and mass. *Elf Quest* was one of the comics that she and Maxx Powers had talked about when they first met in San Francisco, and of course Maxx's *Newt Quest* was his own satirical tribute to WARP Graphics – Wendy and Richard Pini. Fumié was also able to support this device with lettering, employing the cursive, feminine hiragana, traditionally used by Japanese women writers since the Heian Era, along with the sharp, heavy and aggressively masculine katakana, which was originally used in formal documents and in modern times for foreign words and expressions.

Dorado-kun also served as an ethical foil to the feminist advocate Chibi Hanako-chan, and he was allowed all the chauvinisms, naïvetés and posturings of the typical male teenager. So often, when they would meet at a café late in the afternoon, after Dorado-kun got out of classes, Chibi Hanako-chan would talk about her latest battle against sexism, militarism or elitism while Dorado-kun would daydream about sodomizing his sexy calligraphy teacher, Yamada-sensei.

Sodomy, in fact, lent itself to Japanese porn and erotica since the country's quirky censorship laws were pretty much restricted to a ban against depictions of penises and vaginas – cocks and cunts were either blacked out or mosaiced – but assholes were fair game, as were penises for that matter as long as they were in the disembodied form of dildoes or other like objects or sex toys.

Another object of Dorado-kun's sexual fantasies was the tribe of *yamamba* – literally "mountain hags" – the young girls with tanning studio darkened faces highlighted by white lipstick and eye-shadow and favoring pleated tartan mini-skirts and super-high platform-heel boots. But in these fantasies, the *yamamba* were usually sucking his mosaiced cock.

Yet, when the chips were down, Dorado-kun, like Batman's Robin or the Lone Ranger's Tonto, would come out of the shadows of troubled adolescence, a sensitive and powerful New Age Guy, distracting the commuter train groper while Chibi Hanako-chan pick-pocketed his wallet and cell phone, or helping Chibi Hanako-chan break up the assignation between the horny salaryman and the mini-skirted, Louis Vuitton designer handbag carrying high school prostitute at a sleazy riverside love hotel.

Then, unlike Superman and Lois Lane, the couple would retire to their secret hideout in the wilds of western Tokyo and make out furiously, cock and cunt decorously mosaiced out in conformance to Japanese law. In fact, subtly turning the standard mosaic into a camouflaged, puzzle-picture, porno mini-montage was one of the unique and popular features of *Chibi Hanako-chan* manga and led to a noticeable spike in the sale of magnifying glasses among her habitual readers. And the fact that one of Dorado-kun's favorite fantasy sex-objects was his calligraphy teacher gave Fumié the chance to work in a good deal of *kanji* – the Chinese-derived pictographs with which most Japanese is written – and to perpetrate humorous *kanji* double and triple entendres.

*   *   *

As he crossed the border into Washington, to return his rented van and fly back to Mexico, Maxx Powers conducted an ethical debate with himself regarding the future of *Newt Quest*. Originally, he saw the newts much the same as Capek saw them – symbols of the over-exploited working class – enslaved and treated no better than robots, a word which Capek had coined in his play *R.U.R.*, by the humans, who symbolized the ruling class.

When he started writing and drawing *Newt Quest*, Maxx saw it as a social-democratic allegory, with the newts, humble amphibians, struggling to improve their lot in a world dominated by arrogant eagles, boorish bears, vicious vipers, philosophical frogs and – saving, in his opinion, the best for last – mundane but malevolent mice. But now, following the debacle in San Jose over *The Khagans of the Khazars* and *Jesus Christ, Robo-biker*, Maxx Powers was wrestling with the temptation to sell out...to turn the newts into cutesy characters aimed at the eight to ten year old Video Game playing demographic, and their activities into mindless, plot-less adventures complete with stylized violence, unprincipled villains (he could quite honestly relish millions of entry-level Game players ruthlessly massacring legions of vermin infested mice)...to the fast-track building up of a fan base among the elementary school thumb-wankers with a Comics Code approved approach to the newts.

Once on the plane to La Paz, sipping a cool Margarita, Maxx Powers remembered an early manga drawing that Fumié had shown him. It was one she'd done while still a student in Seattle. She had just recently met the Old Man, and had gone off for a weekend with him to one of the San Juan Islands. They stayed at a rustic B & B and one morning, while having coffee out on the patio, had observed a fascinating battle between a newt and a centipede.

The newt was the predator and at first aggressively and confidently attacked what it must have seen as a feast of Dionysian proportions. The feast, however, was more accurately a beast, stinging or pinching the newt repeatedly every time it attacked. Eventually, the newt gave up, probably lucky to be still able to retreat, and the centipede disappeared in a flash into a crack in the flagstones, while the newt crawled away under the overhang of the porch roof.

The drawing was technically rather simple, but the construction of the frames — curves and semi-circles as well as boxes — and the interior monologues of the characters, rendered in thought bubbles, gave it an undeniable charm.

The first five issues of *Newt Quest* were aimed at the young adult audience, especially young adult males. Unlike Karel Capek's newts, who were a previously undiscovered race of intelligent marine amphibians, nearly equal in size to humans, Maxx Powers' newts were standard size red newts, about the same size as a praying mantis, although Maxx had made plans to, at some point in the not-too-distant future, introduce the giant salamanders who lived in some of the mountain-bred rivers of central Japan.

The world of *Newt Quest* was parallel to the world of a modern capitalist society. Eagles were CEO's of giant multi-forest conglomerates, lofty in their professed ideals, graceful in their public appearances, but basically carrion-eating scavengers, not a whole lot better than buzzards in their table manners.

The bald eagles were inevitably North American, while the sea eagles were Japanese, the golden eagles Europeans and so on. Their corporate hench-beasts took many forms – usually raptors and predators or other less visually appealing bottom feeders like crows, sharks and mice. The criminal classes and politicians were mostly made up of rats.

Far away from the bustling, polluted world of commerce and crime, industry and militarism, lived the legendary, perhaps mythical Philosopher Frog Prince, who sat on a lotus leaf in a hidden alpine lake somewhere in an un-named mountain range. The Philosopher Frog Prince held the secret of Transcendence Beyond Samsara, and access to this secret offered the newts, lowly laborers like those in Capek's novel, the means to escape both bodily and spiritually from their oppressed position in the world.

Unlike the typical seeker of social justice in the comics world, the newts were not prone to violence, nor did they possess any super powers, other than perhaps keener than average perceptions and Siddharthian powers of patience and thought, as well as the ability to eschew eating for long periods of time.

In a series of adventures more or less copped from the stories of Chuang Tsu and other "Zen lunatics", but distorted in Borgesian fashion, one intrepid band of newts leaves their small woodland pond on an island off the northwest coast of North America, and begins their spiritual odyssey, hoping to gain audience with their fellow amphibian, the Philosopher Frog Prince.

*　　　　*　　　　*

Jorge Luis Valenzuela was, of course, as he rode his 750cc Kawasaki Zephyr motorcycle down the peninsula towards Todos Santos totally unaware that Maxx Powers, the creator of *Newt Quest*, had been thwarted in his own personal quest for a computer Game contract and would soon be plotting the bastardization of Jorge Luis' favorite comix. Instead, the Silver Surfer of Todos Santos was thinking of nothing more than catching a few waves, taking some long siestas and drinking a few *cervezas* at one of the many beachfront cantinas. He had two days off before his presence would be required back in Puerto San Carlos aboard the Mexican fishing vessel *Los Derechos del Hombre*.

And it was at one of these beachside surfer bars that Jorge Luis Valenzuela, the Silver Surfer of Todos Santos met Fumié Akahoshi, the illustrious Japanese cartoonist, creator of the famous manga, *Chibi Hanako-chan*.

It was a most unlikely meeting. Saddled with the responsibility of caring for an emerging rug rat, not yet two years old, and with her husband and co-parent Maxx Powers annoyingly absent, Fumié had scant time and scarce opportunity to enjoy an evening out drinking at a bar. But on the very same evening that Maxx Powers was spending his last 18 hours on Vancouver Island before finally deciding to head back to Mexico, resolved to alter his financial situation for the better by radically reforming his latest comix, Fumié entrusted the care of their son Bird to a teenage babysitter, one Estella de los Ochos, who she often saw on the beach and who seemed reliable and trustworthy, as well as in need of the few pesos she could earn by spending a few hours with baby Bird in the rich Japanese woman's casa.

Although he was too young to legally drink in a bar, Jorge Luis' mature demeanor, not to mention a head full of silver-gray hair, usually pre-empted any requests on the part of bouncers or bartenders to look at his I.D. Once inside, since it was in his nature to avoid attracting any unwanted attention his vibrant yet outlandish good looks might instigate, and since he knew few of the locals old enough to be there, he usually sat quietly in the shadows, nursing a cold can of beer.

Fumié Akahoshi drifted to the back of the bar, almost out of habit, a habit formed as she became a more recognizable public figure back in Japan, due to her increasingly frequent appearances as a *terebi tarento*. Even here in Todos Santos where she had no fans or follwers, she was still fairly easy to spot, known locally as "la rica japona"...the rich Japanese woman, so she instinctively acted cautiously when alone in public.

Although he was a dedicated *Newt Quest* fan, and perhaps knew, somewhere back in the comix trivia compartment of his brain that Maxx Powers' wife was also a comic book artist in Japan, Jorge Luis Valenzuela made no connection with the attractive older Asian woman moving, beer bottle in hand, toward his darkened corner of the otherwise sunny beachfront cantina, and Maxx Powers, the author of *Newt Quest*.

Fumié Akahoshi, for her part, was carrying, in addition to a cold bottle of Negra Modelo beer, her notebook and a set of drawing pencils, intending to sketch out possible new characters for a possible new manga she had in mind. After all, if Maxx could break the vacation rules they'd made together, well, so could she...

Recently, a new controversy had emerged, involving two

Japanese media giants, the *Asahi Shimbun,* one of Japan's oldest and most respected newspapers, and NHK, the state-run TV network, as well as Japan's long dominant and ruling political party, the LDP. The conflict arose out of a report in the *Asahi* which alleged that a couple of leading LDP legislators, including one obviously being groomed as the next party president, which would inevitably lead him to the position of Prime Minister in Japan's virtually one-party system, had pressured NHK to change the contents of an historical documentary aired on its General TV channel and which exposed the role of Hirohito, the Showa Emperor, in the practice of forcing Chinese, Korean, Filipina and other Asian women into prostitution, or more accurately, sexual slavery, for the Japanese Imperial forces in the 1930's & '40's. It was only adding insult to injury that in the euphemistic language of propaganda, these unfortunate victims were called "comfort women".

Both NHK and the LDP, predictably, reacted in anger and (most likely simulated) outrage and in a scattershot volley of ultimatums, peppered the newspaper with demands that it apologize for and retract the story, reveal its sources, defend its research procedures and everything else short of declaring itself bankrupt (both morally and financially) and closing up shop. *The Asahi Shimbun*, for its part, largely ignored the bluster from the right, simply stating that it stood by its story and refused to embroil itself in the imbroglio.

NHK, however, drove its Toyota to the brink of the abyss of absurdity when it broadcast its plan to cancel live coverage of the National Rugby Championships because the referees would be wearing the logo of one of the game's sponsors, *The Asahi Shimbun*, on their official uniform shirts, a common practice throughout the increasingly corporate world of sports.

There was also a sidebar that the LDP – in effect, the government – was applying pressure on the BBC to alter the contents of a documentary they were putting together on Emperor Hirohito and his role in World War II. The main bone of contention here, however, wasn't the issue of sexual slavery, but rather the Showa Emperor's share of responsibility for the great redundancy of the war, the atomic bombing of Nagasaki. Years earlier, a Nagasaki mayor had been shot by a Right-winger for expressing similar opinions.

Well, these were pretty heavy matters for a girl on her own in a bar in Mexico, Fumié thought, even if the matters might lead eventually to a comic book. But the shiny beer can, tipped in her direction as a toast, the bright black eyes of the young man offering the toast, and his puzzlingly American accented "*konnichiwa*" brought a smile to her face and banished all thoughts of political and moral corruption 60 or 70 or 75 years ago, in countries far, far away.

"It's too late in the day for '*konnichiwa*.' You have to say '*kombanwa*' – 'good evening' not 'good afternoon'... '*buenos tardes*' not '*buenos dias*'."

She tipped her bottle of Negra Modelo toward him, then, taking a step in the direction of his shadowy table, clinked the bottle against the can he was holding. "*Kampai!* That's how you make a toast in Japanese. *Kampai!*"

"*Kampai* then," replied the Silver Surfer of Todos Santos.

*   *   *

Maxx Powers returned to Todos Santos the next day and Fumié tried to pick up where they'd left off as a couple, and as a family with Bird. Things were a little shaky at first, but Fumié went out of her way to show a lot of interest in Maxx's journeys – economical, geographical and ethical – hoping it would distract him from any suspicions about her behavior during his self-imposed exile. Jorge Luis Valenzuela had returned to Puerto San Carlos and was out on *Los Derechos del Hombre* fishing for albacora, bonito and dorado.

The last few days of their holiday took on the warm glow that the trip was intended to imbue, with golden hours spent together on the beach, swimming in the warm Pacific Ocean, building sand castles for little Bird to alight on and then tear down, lounging in the cool of their air-conditioned casa late at night and watching the sickle-shaped moon fall into the silvered sea.

They took a day trip to La Paz to view to Gulf of California or, as the Mexicans preferred to call it, the Sea of Cortez. That night, back in Todos Santos, Fumié got Maxx high on some powerful Mexican marijuana that she'd scored in one of the surfer bars and proceeded to give Maxx the best blow job he could ever remember, fellatio being a treat his wife did not give lightly or freely. She then got him so drunk on tequila that he'd never remember what happened – or didn't happen – next.

*　　　　*　　　　*

Back in Tokyo, Maxx Powers and Fumié Akahoshi collaborated on their first satire of the Imperial Household, a one-off, four-page story called "Harry, Hiro & Dolph" which appeared simultaneously in English in *Heavy Metal* and in Japanese in *Big Comic*. In this realistically illustrated story President Truman, the Showa Emperor and the Fuhrer are depicted on trial in Hell for the war crime of "Atrocious Redundancy" – the atomic bombing of Nagasaki. When Mephistopheles, acting as Hitler's attorney, asks why his client is being brought before the court since he committed suicide several months prior to the atrocity in question, Satan, the Presiding Judge, answers that since Adolph has been designated "The Mother-Fucker of all Atrocities," he is automatically indicted for any and all war crimes or crimes against humanity. In this case, however, since, despite various conspiracy theories and "Elvis sightings" over the years, the accused has been legally declared dead, the charges of responsibility for or complicity in the Nagasaki bombing would summarily be dismissed.

So the trial begins.

The international controversy stirred up by "Harry, Hiro & Dolph," coming as it did during the 60th anniversary of the atomic bombings, stamped Maxx Powers with enough credibility in the world of social and political satire to deflect attention from the increasing infantilization of *Newt Quest* – part of Maxx's personal quest to see one of his comix creations immortalized as a Game, in this case one directed at the lucrative 8-10 year-old, gender non-specific market. The newts suddenly added weapons to their original arsenal of merely physical, intellectual or spiritual powers.

Jorge Luis Valenzuela was not the only *Newt Quest* fan to feel disturbed, puzzled, betrayed and ultimately ripped off by frame after frame of incongruously caped and booted newts blasting venomous vipers with darts with exploding war-heads or trapping and dismembering Gila monsters, giant salamanders and Komodo dragons in camouflaged pits dug along their sacred path to the now largely redundant Philosopher Frog Prince. Indeed, the Silver Surfer of Todos Santos fully expected to soon see the PFP metamorphosize into Galactus, Mephisto or even The Joker.

The eyes of the female newts grew noticeably larger and they began to acquire cute mini-skirted uniforms which, however, were equipped with a variety of cleverly hidden pockets holding a broad range of Ninja-style throwing weapons which they never hesitated to launch at overhanging Black Widows, helicoptering Dragonflies or dive-bombing Tse Tse flies. The deconstruction of *Newt Quest* was in full bellow.

Long Life

The Old Man and the boy returned to Baseball Beach. He still thought of his son as the boy, even though he was now almost forty years old and indeed had a name, Ichiro. There were still a lot of baseballs on the beach. The Tamagawa River still flowed, inexorably coursing toward its perpetual denouement into Tokyo Bay and ultimate climax in the Pacific Ocean.

Neither Ichiro nor the Old Man were what you could call rich, having sunk most of the Old Man's money into growing organic coffee on Hawaii Island, an increasingly competitive business which, for them, was only just beginning to become profitable after years of loss and learning. But now, at age 84, the Old Man had won the Nobel Prize for his novel *The 124 Year Old Man* which, after years of being constantly minimalized toward the goal of being the ultimate short story, had finally burst its dams, overflowed its dykes and flooded hundreds of pages with its inscrutable insights into the human condition and an ironic undertone which kept a reader always on the edge of all-out laughter that was never fully provoked.

Another irony was the fact that the Nobel Prize, while carrying a cash award of $1 Million, was no longer the top-rung award for cultural, diplomatic or scientific achievement. A dozen or so years earlier the Einstein Prizes had been jointly established by the United States, Canada, Israel, Germany and Japan, and carried cash awards of $50 Million, precipitating the Nobel's slide into a relatively minor category, something like the Pulitzer Prize, or the Akutagawa Prize or the Governor General's Award. But it was on this money that the Old Man and his son traveled back to Baseball Beach on the Tamagawa, just across the river from Tokyo.

The dramatic tension in the prize-winning novel *The 124 Year Old Man*, came from an obscure model of mystical numerology, the Theory of Metonic Cycles. This system of thought, which the novel hints may have originated with students of the Kabala, divides the ideal human lifespan into seven 19 year cycles, allowing that 19 years be considered a generation. The first cycle runs from birth to one's 19th birthday...childhood. Next, from 19-38, youth. Then, maturity, 38-57. After that, from 57-76, middle age. Following, elderhood, 76-95. Then, old age, 95-114. Finally, transcendence, or Long Life, 114-133.

The numerological values of each transitional age line up thus:

$$19 = 1+9 = 10 = 1+0 = 1$$
$$38 = 3+8 = 11 = 1+1 = 2$$
$$57 = 5+7 = 12 = 1+2 = 3$$
$$76 = 7+6 = 13 = 1+3 = 4$$
$$95 = 9+5 = 14 = 1+4 = 5$$
$$114 = 1 + 1 + 4 \quad = 6$$
$$133 = 1 + 3 + 3 \quad = 7$$

The 124-year-old man who has, due to both internal and external pressures, become committed to his role as a pioneer on the frontier of human longevity and whose life, revealed in the novel by the intricate inter-weavings of flashbacks, narratives of other characters and authorial intrusions, has clearly borne down on him with such heaviness that he longs for nothing more or less than its conclusion.

The numerical value of 124 which, like 133, also equals 7, offers him a possible loophole through which he can escape nine more years of physical, mental, emotional and moral pain (exquisitely revealed, layer by layer, in the novel) already having missed the opportunity for a much earlier exit from the 7th and last Metonic cycle at age 115.

* * *

Over the 20 or so years since the Old Man and the boy had last walked together on Baseball Beach, little had really changed. Typhoons, often followed by floods, temporarily change the river but, as the seasons, like the river itself, push steadily onward, the gravel bars, the islets, the tiny, absurd peninsulas and their trivial little beaches gradually regain their, one would suppose, predestined form, size and shape.

The Old Man and his son were standing on Baseball Beach a day after flooding caused by a recently passed typhoon. The typhoon had, in fact, delayed their flight into Tokyo and they'd spent an uncomfortable night, considering their recently acquired status as millionaires, in JAL's Executive Class lounge in Honolulu airport, nibbling on cheese and Japanese *senbei* crackers and drinking too much free beer, green tea and machine-made coffee.

The roar of the river a day after flooding dominates all the senses, heightens the acrid, clay-filled odor of mud carried down from the mountains. The flood had washed most of the baseballs from the beach, and those few remaining were stranded along the edges of the peninsula, now grown to twice its normal size due to the huge deposits of mud, gravel, silt and debris. As the Old Man stooped to pick up a muddy baseball to rinse and toss to his now grown and graying son, his eye was captured by another figure on the otherwise empty beach...a black plastic action figure with yellow insect eyes.

Neither the Old Man nor Ichiro could name the action figure, but seemed to recall him from a 1970's era Japanese TV series which they had watched together in re-runs in the '90's. He was just another redundant costumed superhero, of ambiguous motives and morals, simply and illogically possessed of strange powers no longer valued. *Washed up here on the beach, he wants to be resuscitated,* the Old Man imagined...*brought back to life and relevance somewhere*...maybe even in a novel.

The figure wore black tights and body armor, against which the yellow insect eyes stood out with terrible hypnotic power, evoking in the Old Man a fear like the high-pitched whine of a racing Japanese motorcycle on a narrow nighttime street.

The Old Man picked the figure up out of the mud, leaving a baseball a few feet away untouched. He thought of the river on quiet days, rolling and roiling over small smooth boulders, and the hum of traffic from the thoroughfares of Tokyo's Setagaya ward across the water, a drone to which the river could improvise a melody. Sometimes, as if by miraculous transubstantiation of angels, a saxophone solo would wail above the river rhythm from behind the cavernous pilings of the Marukobashi Bridge, the bass line carried by the plunging chords of the torrent over the Chofuseki Dam. A string section emerged from the beating of swallows' wings. The Old Man threw the action figure as far as his 84-year-old arm could send him, until he heard a tiny splash — a brief plop — a modest number of yards from shore. Then, he picked up a flotsam baseball, rinsed off the mud at the river's edge, and gamely tossed it to his son.

*   *   *

Once back in Tokyo, Fumié found she could not stop thinking about Jorge Luis Valenzuela, the young Silver Surfer of Todos Santos. And several weeks later, two missed periods alerted her to the fact that she was likely carrying a permanent reminder of their fleeting night of frenzied passion on the still warm sands of a tropical Mexican beach.

Maxx Powers, once back in Tokyo, suddenly realized that Japanese taxi drivers, like mice, cats, ducks and dogs in American comic books, all wear white gloves. But that while all of the funny animals had four digits on each hand, most of the taxi drivers had five.

*   *   *

When Fumié Akahoshi bought her dream house in Den-en-chofu and moved into this prestigious neighborhood with Maxx Powers and Bird, she was a traditional enough Japanese to make the rounds of the neighbors' houses bearing *hikkoshi aisatsu*, introduction gifts. There was actually a satisfying routine surrounding this practice. You knock on your neighbor's door, or ring the bell. The neighbor answers the door. You bow deeply and recite, almost ritually, the formula: "I'm sorry, please excuse me for disturbing you, but I'm your new neighbor, Akahoshi Fumié; would you please favor me by accepting this small gift." Then you hand the neighbor a box of expensive Japanese *senbei* crackers or Swiss chocolates or assorted gourmet cookies. Then the neighbor bows slightly and replies: "Thank you very much." Finally, you both bow again the required number and depth of bows, taking care not to knock each other on the head, and off you go to the next house.

Fumié, not being too complete a conformist, had brought back bottles of tequila and gift wrapped boxes of dried tropical fruits and smoked albacore white meat tuna. She'd gone around the block counter clockwise and coming back to 1 o'clock, her next door neighbor on the right was the last one she had to visit. But here, when the heavy, dark wooden door opened, a striking, feline, thin-as-a rapier black haired woman dressed in what Fumié first perceived as black pajamas, immediately and urgently beckoned her inside. Somewhat confused by the unorthodox and unexpected invitation, but with an artist's curiosity over-riding caution or formality, she found herself rapidly removing her red leather boots in a spacious *genkan*, bright with recessed lighting and blonde wood paneling, comfortable benches of yellowish cypress wood set off against the gleaming black opalesque tiling of the floor.

"I've been watching you going around the neighborhood," said the woman in black. "I know that you recently bought the house next door...the one that used to belong to *Yokozuna* Shimonoyama, the unfortunate Sumo Grand Champion.... Well, don't be shy. Excuse me please, but since I've been watching you all afternoon, I feel like I already know you...like we've already met. Does that sound strange to you...weird?"

"Well...do you...you're not a stalker surely..."

"Yes, I know who you are. You're Akahoshi Fumié, the creator of *Chibi Hanako-chan*. How could I help but know you? You or your images are on television every day."

"Well, maybe you're the type that doesn't watch TV."

"Unfortunately, I'm not that type. I watch all the soaps religiously, both the after-lunch short dramas and the full length evening dramas. Actually, I'm quite addicted, but I rationalize my nasty little habit as research...for my work."

"So why were you giving up your programs by watching me? Were you expecting to see something dramatic?"

"Well, one never knows, does one?"

"So, since you've already mentioned it, what sort of work do you do, Kamishita-san? You see I noticed your name on your mail slot...and that you write your given name in katakana – Mango. That's...rather melodramatic, wouldn't you say? And by the way, is Mango your husband's name or yours?"

"Well, if I were a manga artist or had a husband, I suppose it would be melodramatic...or worse. But I'm definitely not an artist."

"But your work, whatever it is, must be quite lucrative for you to own such a large beautiful home here in Den-en-chofu...or...did you...inherit it?"

"I did, as a matter of fact, inherit this house, the house I was born in. My parents died, quite dramatically, a few years ago in Egypt...gunned down by what the TV news calls 'terrorists'."

"Oh! I'm very sorry. Please forgive me for my insensitive question...I had no idea. Do you mean to say that they were among the group of Japanese tourists massacred while visiting the pyramids?"

"Yes, that's right. But my work is quite lucrative, as you say. The taxes alone on a house like this demand it."

"So..."

"Like you, I'm a writer. But you aren't likely to see my name on a book, because I only use pen-names."

"Well then, would I know you by one or more of your pen-names?"

"Only if you're an avid reader of women's porn novels. I write those little pocket-size books, the one's with a few stylized picture pages and stories of bondage, costume play, office depravity...you know the ones...don't you?"

"So! Well, I'm not an avid reader, but yes, I do know them and I must admit I have a few...for research...ha, ha, ha...although I've never paid too much attention to the author's names."

"Certainly there's no reason to. Nor do I...pay much attention to them, that is. I keep them quite generic – Keiko Kato, Yuki Abe, Ai Suzuki – short, easy to recognize, non-threatening – you want your readers to keep coming back, isn't that right?"

"Yes it is," said Fumié. "Certainly."

*   *   *

Back at their hotel in Shinjuku, the Old Man, at 84 old enough to be his son's grandfather, rested, while Ichiro, who'd managed to contact a few of his former baseball teammates from 30 years or more past, was out with them tearing up the town, at least in the manner of ex-boys now approaching 40. The Old Man was thinking about a section in his Nobel Prize-winning novel, *The 124 Year Old Man*, the instrument which provided the dough-re-mi to pay for this ridiculously overpriced, albeit luxurious hotel room, the section where the 124-year-old man thinks of his ninety-something-year-old son thinking of his sixty-something-year-old son (the 124-year-old man's grandson) waiting ever more impatiently for him (the sixty-something's father, the 124-year-old man's son) to just get it over with and die. *What*, he wondered, with a faint, but ever-increasing sense of dread, *was his thirty-some-thing-year-old son thinking...if anything...about him?*

*　　　　*　　　　*

Jorge Luis Valenzuela, who was now the same age that the Old Man's son Ichiro was during the pair's Nobel Prize financed trip to Tokyo, and was, although none of the three parties mentioned above knew it at the time of the Tokyo visit, actually the Old Man's grandson, surfing in the South Pacific Ocean on a typically picturesque South American beach. He was a long way from his birthplace, Hawaii Island, or from Todos Santos, the Mexican beach town in Baja California, both in the North Pacific Ocean where so many melodramatic events had occurred, so many years ago.

There was a comfort in surfing which came from the form and quality of the waves and the overriding state of the sea. There were days when the waves here were nothing more than memories of the great waves on those legendary, nay epic days so long ago and so far away. Days full of sunshine, sharks and blood. On other days, the waves simply repeated the mind-emptying drone of surf breaking on the beach, the soul cleansing rhythm of the rise and fall of the sea, the pervasive aura of peace as the sun met the horizon in a riot of unworldly color, culminating in the *satori* of the green flash on the eyes' edge as the sun retreated into its underwater caverns for the night. On days like this, the Silver Surfer of Todos Santos could relax a little and take comfort in being able to more or less blend in with the regular gang of surfers on this typically picturesque South American beach.

*   *   *

A generation before the Silver Surfer of Todos Santos found himself fetched up in South America, the Old Man had begun his Nobel Prize-winning novel thus:

The Guinness Book of World Records had declared him the world's oldest living human.

He was not sure exactly where it was that he was now living. He knew he'd been born in Canada and in fact he often recalled scenes, some unbearably painful, others quite full of adventure and delight, from 120 or even 121 years earlier. He was told that he'd spent 25 years in Europe and another 25 in Asia, but those 50 years, from his late twenties to seventies usually only came to him as a blur of random vignettes...somewhere big cedar trees and a forest path...somewhere the roar and blare of city traffic at Rush Hour...somewhere a beach with small waves on an inland sea....

He was now, he felt quite sure, in a tropical or subtropical location, perhaps on an island or peninsula, and likely very near a beach, as he could smell the salt tang of the ocean strongly, every day. He enjoyed the smell and it gave him something to look forward to.

Perhaps he had even been to the beach, but there had been so many beaches, so far away...Thailand, Jamaica, Nova Scotia, Brazil, Borneo, Hokkaido, Australia, Alabama, some tropical and lush, some cold and sere, and so he could only be sure he was near a warm beach now. He was lightly clothed in a brightly colored short-sleeved shirt and some khaki cotton shorts. He was barefoot, and there was a thin pair of rubber zori at his feet.

He was, it seemed to him, sitting in a garden in hot, sunny weather, under the dark green foliage of a large, spreading tree, and he could smell several kinds of fruit... sweet smelling fruit like guava, or papaya or tangerine. *Tangerine...mikan...mandarin...Japanese orange*...he wasn't really sure what to call whatever it was he was smelling...because he wasn't really sure where the hell he was.

He knew that once he had a daughter who lived in Hawaii, on the Big Island, but if she were alive today she'd be over 90, so he didn't think he'd be living with her. Her name was a flower, or maybe it was an animal, like Cat, or Raven...no, it was Camille, like the flower camellia, or was that her grand daughter's name. Yes, Camille, his great-grand -daughter. An old woman in her sixties. That's where he must be living. With her. But where did she live? Was it still Hawaii? Was he on or off the beach?

*   *   *

Fumié Akahoshi and Mango Kamishita had developed a close friendship over the next couple of years, so it was Mango that Fumié sought out to confide in and confess the news of her latest pregnancy, and her torrid yet truncated affair with Jorge Luis Valenzuela, the Silver Surfer of Todos Santos. It was in Mango's spacious living room, sipping Mango's homemade *ume-shu* plum liqueur that Fumié told Mango her tale.

It was inevitable that this audience with Mango Kamishita take place in Mango's house, because Mango rarely, if ever, left it, being severely agoraphobic. She would become intensely anxious and agitated at the thought of being forced or required to leave her lavish sanctuary and face the streets of Tokyo, even such streets as benign and comfortably residential as Den-en-chofu.

So Mango created her own world, her pleasure dome, within the commodious confines of her deceased parents' magnificent mansion. The building's interior swam with house plants, gliding on, over and around its surface, an expanse of green and white striped vines and tendrils, green-edged broad and thin purple leaves, riotous red and orange flowers, with delicate yellow challengers to their visual supremacy peeking out from behind the fibrous trunks of various potted palms, and cacti flourishing in dry patterns in front of sun-splashed deserts of rice straw *tatami* mats.

Her living room was on the second floor and was fronted by a long, wide balcony, which ran the room's entire length outside its south facing sliding glass doors. The foreground view was into a walled garden, about average size for this neighborhood, not breathtakingly large, but by no means modest. In a style both typical and traditional, the garden contained mostly trees – flowering, fruit-bearing, symbolic and ornamental.

The pines (*matsu*) were trained, limbs straightened and directed in the desired direction, bound by galvanized iron wire over weathered bamboo braces, like metal braces on the handicapped legs of a malformed child.

One magnificent old *sakura* cherry, there for its blossoms only as it bore no fruit, stood just west of center, with enough bare ground around it for a *hanami* party in the late March cherry-viewing season.

The fruit trees were the Japanese *ume* plum, used to make a supply of *ume shu* liqueur, and whose February blossoms pointed the way to spring in the coldest month of the year; persimmon, or *kaki*, which blossomed in the fall and whose rich orange fruit clung to its bare black branches right into December; loquats, or *biwa*, whose small yellow fruits cut through the long gray days of the rainy season in late June and early July.

There was a small grove of tall bamboo and a row of short ornamental cedar bracketed on either end by soaring, blue-green Himalayan cedar.

The seasonal flowers were also prominent, with delicate yellow narcissus and daffodils yielding to bold tulips in a variety of strong hues, watched over by both white and purple magnolias as spring progressed. Summer brought lacy lavender clusters of wisteria and scarlet hibiscus with lewd, laughing yellow tongues and autumn the giant chrysanthemums in chrome yellow, pale purple and pure white. Blood red and erotic pink camellias dominated the winter garden.

Fumié saw all this and more in her memories and imagination as the garden vista beyond the balcony carried her, as if on a carpet out of the Arabian Nights, beyond the borders of the here and now and back to her childhood and to the precious hours in the art room at her school...before Principal Takayama-*sensei* changed all that.

∗   ∗   ∗

"What a great plot!" Mango said, "giving her husband the greatest blowjob of his life and then getting him so drunk he won't remember anything else about the night, and all to cover up her getting pregnant from a one-night stand the night before and forever convince him that the child is his. I don't think I'd've gotten that off the afternoon soaps, but it reminds me of one of those kinky Bible stories from the show your ex used to write...what was it called?"

"We're No Angels."

"Right...and *We're No Saints.* I'm gonna steal this from

you of course, but no worries...I'll change everything...ages, locations...everything."

"We're no saints!"

* * *

When the baby girl was born a few months later, they called her Angelica. Angelica Akahoshi. Spending more time at home in Den-en-chofu with a newborn and a rugrat to care for, Fumié spent most of her hours of freedom creating and producing edgier and more political manga and less time in the public eye on TV. She also spent more time just thinking, and the more she thought about Japan's increasingly right-wing tendencies – sending the "Self Defense Forces" to help occupy Iraq; privatizing government services like the post office and highways department; lobbying to change the Constitution, especially the war-renouncing Article 9; refusing to compensate "comfort women" and other war-time victims; enshrining convicted war criminals in the infamous Yasukuni Shrine and suggesting the Emperor go there to pay his respects; resisting popular calls for female members of the Imperial Family to ascend to the throne – the more she wanted to confront both Japan's past history and future possibility in a scathingly satirical manga...to give the injustice of privilege and the arrogance of power the pictorial and literary tongue lashing she felt they righteously deserved.

Originally, her plan was to create a story where a Japanese Emperor is discovered to be keeping a harem of both young male and female Filipino sex slaves in isolation in a secret chamber of the Imperial Palace. He will have gotten the sex slaves from the fabulously wealthy sultan of an oil-rich southeast Asian state. She decided on this particular sultan after reading that he'd had Michael Jackson sing at his 50th birthday party gala.

The story would be published in the *Gomi ga shima* manga so that the characters could be suitably portrayed as personified birds and insects, rather than as actual human beings. The sex slaves would of course be cicadas, the males gaily chirping away, the females typically silent. The Emperor could be an Imperial eagle or a pheasant, the Japanese national bird, or a majestic crane, the symbol of happiness. The Sultan, head of a huge human trafficking ring, could be a powerful pelagic albatross.

But, perhaps because of her paralyzing indecision about which bird the Emperor should be, she eventually took the fateful step of presenting the story in *Chibi Hanako-chan*. The plot was simple enough. Using the "Chibi Hanako-chan in the 5th Dimension" format, which she had so successfully employed in her famous cancer-defeating *Alpha Mind Control Comics*, Chibi Hanako-chan goes through a time/space warp to a parallel universe, which exists as a distorted mirror-image to our own. There is, of course, a parallel Japan – *Mangetsu* – which is a distorted reflection of the history, geography, government and Imperial Family of the actual Japan. Nevertheless, Mangetsu could be perceived as being consistent enough with reality to be an anathema to certain sinister and powerful segments of the Japanese population.

*   *   *

Another topic that Fumié Akahoshi thought about during this time was parentage. Although divorced from the Old Man and married to Maxx Powers, Fumié continued her relationship with her first husband through a long and increasingly intimate correspondence. The Old Man had revealed to her the subject of the troubling dreams he'd been having around the time that she appeared in Hawaii during his "do nothing/write nothing" year to irrevocably alter his life as a married man. She had written to him about her continuing passion for painting colorful flowers and in fact one of her "trademarks" in *Chibi Hanako-chan* was to include a drawing of an appropriate seasonal flower on one of the four slick-paper color pages that preceded the black & white pulp-paper pages which make up the bulk of Japanese manga magazines. The mention of *asagao* – morning glory – triggered a flood of images in the Old Man's memory and he wrote back recalling the story of a one-night stand in Big Sur in the 1960's with a young hippie chick who called herself Morning Glory. He himself had been using the name Dragonfly. It was possible that Dragonfly had gotten Morning Glory pregnant and that the unknown son who haunted the Old Man in the dream was also hers.

Fumié remembered that Maxx Powers once told her that his mother, Gloria Montenegro, had, in her youth, gone by the nickname Morning Glory. She also remembered that Gloria had given Maxx the nickname "Powers" after he created his first comic, "Dragonflyman," as a boy. Later, on the same day she received this information from the Old Man, she asked Maxx Powers what, if anything, Gloria Montenegro had ever told him about his father.

Maxx Powers told Fumié that Gloria often said that she didn't know for sure who his father was, because as a young flower child in the era of sexual liberation, she had too many sex partners to ever be really sure. But on being pressed, he did remember that he once ran into his mother, who "went nuts" after the disappearance of Max Roach in

Mexico, on the streets of San Francisco, where she was living the rough life of a bag lady. Their conversation had been awkward for both of them, he being unnaturally polite, she being characteristically evasive and cryptic – going as far as to fall into the Serbo-Croatian her own immigrant parents had used at home. When, on parting, he asked if she had any last thoughts on his paternal parentage. At first she just laughed at him and started walking away, pushing her shopping-cart ahead of her, but then she turned briefly and shouted "Mr. Libela!" Maxx could find no "Libela" in the San Francisco telephone book and soon forgot all about it.

Fumié immediately went on the internet and searched for an on-line Serbo-Croatian dictionary. Prepared to be shocked she was not really surprised to discover that "*libela*" was Croatian slang for "dragonfly."

Fumié wrote back to the Old Man with this information, but got no immediate answer. In the meanwhile, she asked Maxx Powers whether he'd ever had a one-night stand. "Yes," Maxx responded, back in his student days, during a spring vacation trip to Mexico. Of course, it was in Baja, on the beach at Todos Santos. Although her heart fell when she realized how insensitive to her feelings Maxx Powers was in choosing this very spot for their vacation together, and not insensitive herself to the potential irony she might reveal by further probing into the matter, she pressed on with her interrogations.

"What do you remember about the girl?" she wanted to know.

"Well, she was Mexican...Mexican-American, I think. She was on vacation too, or something like that. Actually, I think she came from New York, but I really can't say for sure. It was a long time ago and I was pretty young and horny...and pretty drunk, too."

"How about her name...do you remember her name?"

"I think so...but what's so important about it anyway?"

"I'm curious. Do you remember her name?"

"She had a regular Spanish name, but she called herself 'Becky'...that's how I remember that she came from the States."

"How about her last name...?"

"Gee...I don't know. I think it sounded like a country in South America."

"Really...like what...? Columbo? Brazil?"

"No, no... Venezuela...something like that...Becky Venezuela."

*   *   *

In her manga, the sly, suave and scheming younger brother of Tomohito, the Crown Prince of Mangetsu arranges, through the highest echelons of the Mangetsuese *yakuza* hierarchy, to assassinate the legitimate heir by that most traditional method, poison. Bribes are paid, arrangements are made, and the next year, when the old Emperor crosses the bar to the spirit world, exquisitely drawn and lettered in the archaic style of Kazuichi Hanawa, the younger son ascends to the throne.

While the late Crown Prince Tomohito is portrayed as a devoted family man with two young daughters – a rather feeble attempt to fictionalize – and hinted at as being secretly gay, the evil brother is just the opposite – a chauvinist, nationalist, militarist and lecher – a villain right out of the most banal melodramas.

But before this, while the old Emperor lies dying in the Imperial hospital and the old Crown Prince lies dead in his grave, the plot takes a quirky turn. The new Crown Prince, now called Takahito, moves into the palace of his murdered brother and discovers that his minders – the officials of the Imperial Household Agency – have been harboring a secret as dark as the new Crown Prince himself...a harem of young male and female sex slaves from the Isabella Islands, collected and shipped by the Sultan of Tunai.

Chibi Hanako-chan, as readers have long since known, is gifted with the ability to maximize and utilize her psychic powers, which, as readers have long since also known, everyone has, but few know how to use...the same powers so famously and effectively channeled by our heroine in *Alpha Mind Control Comics* through the two stripeless tigers of Asia and Africa. As fate would have it, Chibi Hanako-chan is attending a conference on human trafficking and child sexual abuse in Third World countries being held directly across the road from the Palace at the Canuckian Embassy. The confluence of the intensity of emotion at the conference – long-suffering social workers, pitiable rescued former victims, coldly professional, perhaps even disinterested police – and the proximity of the Imperial perpetrator who is gleefully rejoicing over this unexpected windfall to his ill-begotten inheritance, serves to connect the appropriate psychic synapses in Chibi Hanako-chan's hard-wired brain and she immediately reacts and, eschewing the ubiquitous cell phone, telepathically communicates with her young social injustice fighting cohort, Dorado-kun.

To make a long story short, the two connect at a nondescript ramen shop in Akayama, a nearby middle-class residential neighborhood, and by a fortuitous mix of camouflage, stealth, physical dexterity and the use of Ninja-like psychic powers to distract, disarm and immobilize the palace's formidable security network, enter the palace and, like a John Irving hero in a Vienna zoo, set free the slaves.

In the subsequent issue, the story-line shifts to the agonizing dilemma of the Mangetsuese media – the driving desire to make hay on a sex scandal at the highest level of society, and the all-too-real and present danger of involving in the scandal the god-like denizens of the Imperial Family Household.

Chibi Hanako-chan fans never got to read the issue resolving the dramatic issue of the media and the Imperial Sex Slave Scandal. One night, while Maxx was home and sleeping with her, Bird Powers and Angela Akahoshi asleep in the room next door, two bullets crashed through a window in each room and the throaty roar of a big Kawasaki motorcycle was heard, speeding out of the otherwise silent 4 a.m. streets of Den-en-chofu. Both she and Maxx knew at once that this was a warning. The follow-through would come, just as suddenly, just as violently, just as fast.

Wisdom

Eventually, a great sadness fell, like snow clouds over a weakening winter sun, on the Old Man whenever he remembered his life with Fumié Akahoshi and their son Ichiro. More than anything else, he remembered the hours he and the boy spent together at Baseball Beach along the Tamagawa River while Fumié worked at the Stockholm Massage Clinic in the days before she became famous as the creator of the popular and influential manga *Chibi Hanako-chan*. And those thoughts, eventually, led him to recall the conversations between Fumié and himself, after Ichiro had gone to bed, conversations about the continuing pressure she was feeling from both inside herself and out, to quit the job.

The Baseball Beach memories brought with them a melancholic sadness, a nostalgia which at his age could be easily excused or even enjoyed as a slightly guilty pleasure. But the recollections of the troubles at Stockholm Massage came from much deeper in his psyche, troubling him down to his very soul.

The same year he discovered Baseball Beach and began making his installations, – or "set-ups" as he called them – on the beaches of East Japan, the Old Man also took on the voluntary task of coaching Ichiro's Little League baseball team. The team of 7-11 year-olds was composed of nearly all the "foreign" or "mixed" boys of that age in the Shin Maruko neighborhood. Ichiro was among the youngest, but showed good natural ability, coupled with overwhelming enthusiasm and won himself a position at second base.

Without a large "talent pool" to choose from, concentrations of foreigners or "international" couples with children in Japan being few and often far between, the Old Man depended on simplicity and strategy to make his gang of outsiders competitive with the well-trained, disciplined and highly scrutinized cadres of native Japanese youth. This boiled down to three basic rules and one overall philosophy:

Rule #1 – follow through on every throw

Rule #2 – back up your teammate on every catch

Rule #3 – if the bases are empty, throw the ball "Around the Horn" after every out;

and the Philosophy – "always put the ball in play because then, anything can happen."

*　　　　*　　　　*

Of course, had Fumié not been pressured to provide more and more sexual services with her massages, she, in all likelihood, would never have metamorphosized into Fumié Akahoshi, the rich and famous manga artist, creator of the great liberated Japanese heroine Chibi Hanako-chan. Had she merely continued to do shiatsu and not "relax course" – the one where the "patient" lies on his back while the masseuse oils up and masturbates his erection until he comes, whereupon she cleans him up with a warm, wet *oshibori* towel...or the "prostate health course" – where the masseuse anally penetrates the patient with a greased-rubber-gloved finger and massaging the gland, induces ejaculation "through the back door" – she might still be with him today, comfortably retired, traveling together to the places they talked about so many years ago – Australia, Argentina, Azerbaijan.

The three rules he taught his team, the "Renegades," were defensive tactics and were born of the Old Man's observation through the years that Little Leaguers' most common errors were in the form of wild throws and the subsequent lack of back-up, turning a mere misplay into a minor calamity...a runner who should have been doubled up after a routine fly for an inning-ending out, scoring from first base instead. Rule # 1 decreased the possibility of a bad throw while Rule #2 applied immediate damage control should a poor throw occur anyway. Rule #3 was meant to build enthusiasm, teamwork and communication by involving as many players as possible in each play, as well as promoting individual dexterity and focus – keeping one's eye on the ball. The philosophy was, of course, an offensive strategy.

Kawaguchi-sensei, Fumié's employer, the failed orthopedic surgeon who owned Stockholm Massage, had boosted his market share in the cutthroat environment of the health service business by discreetly expanding into the labyrinthine borderlands of the sex trade...turning Stockholm into more massage parlor than clinic, while maintaining a therapeutic front to keep the establishment's services covered by the National Health Insurance Plan, which routinely paid 70% of a person's medical charges. He hired another female masseuse, Megumi Matsuyama, and divided the clinic into sections.

The front section remained liniment-smelling and crowded with a row of narrow padded cots, a more or less standard room for treating the aching backs, necks and shoulders of overburdened young housewives, time-weary *obasan* – the neighborhood's gaggle of middle-aged women – and the few senior citizens who'd lived in this riverside community long before it had become a somewhat trendy new suburb...a border town between Tokyo and Yokohama.

The back section, however, was divided into several small and private rooms and here the female therapists practiced their ever evolving specialties on the overworked and over-wrought salarymen or local entrepreneurs who came in during lunch hour, or more typically around 9 P.M. The "Copenhagen Room" was the venue for masturbation ("relax course"), while the "Helsinki Room" specialized in stimulating the prostate, a practice widely believed to prevent enlargement of this sensitive male gland, and even to ward off cancer. In any event, it had a large number of devotees.

Fumié and Megumi had several costume options in these secret little rooms. For those who might have a nurse fetish, the girls wore starched white uniforms featuring sheer white pantyhose and mini-skirts. Otherwise, they would strip out of their light blue clinical clothing and down to their underwear, a white or pink bra and a white thong being the most popular. The patients could look all they wanted, but, as in a strip club and unlike the hostess bar, they couldn't touch.

Things often heated up in the Helsinki Room, which was conveniently mirrored so the patient could get a good view of the action going on behind his back. For an extra charge, billed as "chiropractic service" and including optional spanking, the women would don dominatrix gear — black vinyl or leather corsets with push-up bras, red or black fishnet stockings, spike heeled shoes or boots — and the men could be shackled or bound if they wished. The fee was considerably higher for this amenity, which went to pay for the expensive soundproofing the room required. There was even a normal clinical cubicle between these two rooms for those who actually required a therapeutic prostate massage.

But the pot finally boiled over for Fumié when a third girl, Otome Oguchi, was hired and another private quarter, the "Amsterdam Room", was opened for the "full body health course" which was a deluxe working over with scented oils, culminating with a soaping down of the genitals followed by fellatio. Swallowing – "the Parisian treatment" – or a nude masseuse – "the Riviera treatment" – were offered at considerably extra cost, but were quite popular nevertheless...after all, the government was footing 70% of the bill.

At first, Otome Oguchi was the sole operator in the Amsterdam room, but after a while Dr. Kawaguchi proposed a room by room rotation. Fumié and Megumi were already alternating between Copenhagen and Helsinki. Megumi, after some initial resistance, punctuated by a demand for a considerable raise in pay, eventually relented and agreed but Fumié stubbornly continued to refuse. Kawaguchi-*sensei* increasingly applied more pressure, appealing to a sense of fairness, preserving the *wa* or harmony among the clinic staff, and when that didn't work, direct economic measures. While he couldn't cut Fumié's basic salary, he could deny her the bonuses he was now dishing out to Megumi and Otome.

Then one day the dam burst, Fumié returned home from work early and in a flood of tears, and the Old Man stood helplessly by while she cried and cried alone in their bedroom. When Ichiro came home from school, the Old Man told him that Fumié was sick and took him to a nearby rotary sushi bar for dinner and later for what the Old Man was to remember as an exciting adventure for Ichiro – a late night visit to Baseball Beach. They built a campfire and drank a lot of hot oolong tea which they'd brought in a thermos bottle and, unless his memory was now deceiving him, had lit a number of sparklers and even fired off a few starbursts and bottle rockets. And if his reminiscences were indeed correct, their homemade fireworks display was the harbinger of the fantastic new career which lay just around the corner for Fumié.

*   *   *

The warning shots came early in the morning hours, and before the sun could rise, Fumié was on her way to Haneda Airport. Maxx, along with Bird and Angelica, remained at home, the feeling being that Fumié, because of her Imperial scandal cartoons, was the target. They also believed that whoever had ordered and organized the hit – the Japanese Right-wing paramilitaries or their *yakuza* associates – would want a "clean" hit. Kidnapping or further threatening the family of intended victims was not their common modus operandi...at least not at this stage of the game.

On the other hand, the *yakuza's* ability to track and locate a fleeing quarry was frighteningly successful. For this reason, Fumié didn't tell Maxx where she intended to go, if indeed she knew herself when she drove off into the approaching dawn.

Haneda Airport, along the Tokyo side of the Tamagawa, serves domestic flights. It's a lot closer to Den-en-chofu – practically a neighbor – and a lot easier to negotiate, especially at short notice than Narita International Airport. If the *yakuza* were indeed shifting into high gear, this slight attempt at subterfuge – avoiding Narita – would be of little value but, largely playing everything by ear, she caught the early business class flight to Nagoya and there she boarded her first in a long and tiring series of international flights.

The first day in flight was quite literally just that. Nagoya to Cheju, a Korean resort island in the East China Sea and from there to Shanghai, London, Mexico City and finally her settled-upon destination. Furiously drawing manga to consume the supersonic time, Fumié soon realized that there was only one entity on the planet who could and would try to save her...the Silver Surfer.

Jorge Luis Valenzuela, the Silver Surfer of Todos Santos, lover of Fumié Akahoshi, father of her child Angelica Akahoshi, was quite possibly the son of her husband Maxx Powers, following his one-night stand on the beach at Todos Santos twenty years or so earlier with Becky Valenzuela, who was quite possibly the Silver Surfer's mother. Her need to confirm all the facts of this case was as strong as her desire to enlist the Surfer's aid in helping her escape death at the hands of the *yakuza*.

Since she didn't know where in Todos Santos Jorge Luis Valenzuela lived, or whether he was out fishing on *Los Derechos del Hombre*, Fumié, after arriving in Todos Santos on a bus from La Paz, checked into a quiet, downmarket hotel, crawled into bed and crashed, dead to the world, for the next sixteen hours. It was evening when she finally woke up, showered, put on her make up and headed out to the surfside bar where she and the Silver Surfer had first met.

*   *   *

Although not much shocked the Old Man any more – he'd lived too long in the heart of a dying empire to be really surprised about anything – the letter he received from Mango Kamishita, who he'd never met, but who Fumié had often mentioned in her letters, managed to raise his blood pressure and send him scurrying for the couch. Following close on the heels of Fumié's letter identifying him as "Mr. Libela" or "Dragonfly," the father of Maxx Powers (the very man who had taken his place in bed beside his ex-wife Fumié Akahoshi) following his one-night stand on the beach at Big Sur with Maxx's mother Gloria Montenegro, aka "Morning Glory" over forty years past, Mango's missive revealed that Jorge Luis Valenzuela and not Maxx Powers was the father of Fumié's baby Angelica Akahoshi and that Maxx Powers was quite likely the father of Jorge Luis Valenzuela. Leaning back on his sofa with his feet up on a chair for support, the Old Man figured out that Bird Powers and Angelica Akahoshi, the half-siblings of his own son Ichiro were, in reality, his grandson and great-granddaughter. And that his ex-wife Fumié Akahoshi was in fact the mother of them all.

*   *   *

While Fumié Akahoshi was winging her way around the world trying to escape the tentacles of the *yakuza* assassin she knew she would meet somewhere, Maxx Powers was consulting Shomer ben Ghoshi, an international law expert living in Tokyo and in the employ of the Tel Aviv based Israeli mafia, who had close ties with the Japanese *yakuza* in connection with the cadres of Israeli youth who worked the streets of practically every Japanese city as vendors of cheap jewelry and knock-off brand name watches.

While Maxx knew his hopes for Fumié were slim, he also knew that hopes for himself and his children Bird and Angelica, given the right amount of money in the right hands at the right time – the sooner the better – were much better, especially if he were to steer his political lampooning far to the left of the Imperial Family of Japan. Maxx depended on ben Ghoshi to design the financial foundation upon which this hope might be built.

Ben Ghoshi tapped a few keys on his cell phone and fifteen minutes later assured Maxx that he could take his kids and go home. He judiciously avoided any mention of the name Fumié Akahoshi.

*　　　　*　　　　*

Fumié didn't find the Silver Surfer at the surf bar right away, but she did run into her former babysitter Estella de los Ochos, who told her that Jorge Luis was indeed out fishing on *Los Derechos del Hombre* but should be back in port tomorrow morning and more than likely down here in Todos Santos by tomorrow afternoon. She also gave Fumié directions to Jorge Luis' house.

"No," she sighed, "the Silver Surfer didn't carry a cell phone, but perhaps he had an answering machine."

Fumié wandered the streets of Todos Santos most of the night, walking off a considerable load of jet-lag as well as locating the Silver Surfer's casa and walking back to it from all possible directions, fixing various landmarks in her head.

*　　　　*　　　　*

The studded black leather biker jacket hung on a clothes rack in the computer room, the same place it had hung all the while Angelica Akahoshi was growing up, in the fabulously wealthy Tokyo neighborhood of Den-en-chofu. In the home of her adoptive mother – "my cloth monkey" Angelica liked to call her – Mango Kamishita.

Mango never wore the jacket, never even put it on, except once, just to stop bratty Angelica's whining. Since she never left her house, she never had the need to wear it.

Angelica was now considering whether or not to wear it for her TV interview. If she did, it would feel the air of the streets for the first time in nearly a dozen years. That was when she wore it to the first interview, after winning the prestigious Akutagawa Prize for her graphic novel about her life with Mango, *Cloth Monkey*. At thirteen, she was the youngest writer ever to win the prize. Mango had been killed the year before, when Angelica was twelve, and even though she inherited Mango's house, she was more or less forced to live next door with her "father" Maxx Powers and her brother Bird. She went into virtual seclusion in her room for a year and wrote and drew *Cloth Monkey* which became an overnight sensation and sold over a million copies the first year. As if she needed the money.

Now, in her twenties, she had finally completed another graphic novel, this one about the real mother with whom she never had a life and now, 20 years and more after her disappearance, was declared legally dead.

*   *   *

At the headquarters of the Kurotombo-gumi *yakuza* crime organization in Adachi Ward, Tokyo, the Boss, Junichiro Yamasaki, had just gotten the "Commandant", Right-wing big shot Kuroyama out the door with assurances that the matter would be taken seriously and taken care of expediently – and soon, soon, "Now if you'll please excuse me, I'll get right to work on the matter."

Commandant Kuroyama's agitated energy was soon replaced in the office by the calm, mediating presence of the Boss's chief lieutenant, Yutaka Kanzaki. Much to the Boss's surprise, Kanzaki-san had decided on the half-Samoan ex-sumo wrestler Ohsanshouo to assassinate the woman manga artist who they now knew was somewhere in Mexico, where it would be just a short time before they got the precise location from their Mexican mafia associates and their lackeys, the Federales.

Killing a woman, a mother of small children, a comic book writer – despite the facts of her wealth and apparent influence – was beneath the honor of any respect-worthy Japanese – or, for that matter, Korean gang member. But the former *Komusubi* Ohsanshouo, the ultimately disappointing sumotori who, despite his size, his strength and his early promise, failed to rise above the lowest of the three *sanyaku* ranks, the three elite positions just below *Yokozuna*, or Grand Champion, and after one tournament as a Junior Champion, rapidly plunged down the rankings and out of the professional divisions.

Yes, it was said, he had size, strength and even technique, but, it was also said, he lacked concentration, focus, fighting spirit and the ability to think on his feet. He was often beaten by lighter, faster and smarter opponents and after the first few years of winning records, culminating in his promotion to *komusubi,* never achieved a majority of victories in a tournament again.

Ohsanshouo was also a notable failure at his next career, that of a K-1 fighter, pulling out of the "sport" with a record of one win against fifteen humiliating losses.

Nevertheless, he was big, badly in need of money, willing to travel and tough enough to kill a helpless woman.

"And besides," Kanzaki-san laughed, after quickly taking another cell phone call, "Ohsanshouo really likes to surf."

*　　　　*　　　　*

"I could never even get Mango to wear this jacket on the balcony," Angelica Akahoshi had said to the TV hostess during the first interview. "The balcony was the one place she would go to feel the air outside the house. Mango never even went into the walled garden... and no one could even see into the garden from the street. But people said Mango was 'agoraphobic' – that means 'fear of crowds'..."

"I know," said Sato-san, the interviewer.

"And Tokyo's really crowded..."

"I know that too," said Sato-san.

"But she would often go out on the balcony and look into the garden. It was, like, her favorite place to go. She called it her border town, like her house was her country and Den-en-chofu and the rest of Tokyo was another country. The balcony was the border town on her country's side of the border and the garden was the border town of the other country. Mango never even applied for a visa."

"So after your birth mother, Fumié Akahoshi, disappeared, you were taken in by Mango, who was your next-door neighbor and your mother's best friend?"

"Yeah."

"But you were free to come and go like a normal person?"

"Well, at first I was still a baby, but of course, once I got older and started school, I had friends, my Dad Maxx Powers and my brother Bird lived next door...although Maxx spent most of his time at his studio in Roppongi Hills...in 'the Tower'. And so Bird spent a lot of time in the country with his grandparents, the Akahoshi's. Our older brother, Ichiro, spent a lot of time with them too, while Fumié was busy getting rich and famous writing manga and then after she left the Old Man for Maxx Powers, Bird's Dad."

"But Maxx Powers is your Dad too, right?"

"Legally. I like to call him 'the Wire Monkey,' ha, ha, ha."

"Ha, ha, ha."

*   *   *

"*OK, wake up!*" came the command in an un-identifiable accent and Fumié Akahoshi struggled out of a deep sleep to the sight of a massive expanse of cream & coffee-colored flesh. Next, she saw the gun, not unexpectedly, because she smelled something oiled and metallic as soon as she became conscious and awake. And of course she was only too aware that she was a hunted fugitive. So now she expected the shots and then it would be over...even sooner than she had feared. Had she been too careless, or were the *yakuza* connections too far-flung to evade them? Well, she would never know because in another moment, she would be dead.

Ohsanshouo, however, had other ideas. The photo that Kanzaki-san had given him of the target immediately aroused his lust. She was very Asian looking, just the type he liked. Her hair was black and, he guessed, she'd be too busy running to dye it. At least he hoped so. She had the small, flat peasant nose he liked to see on female faces, small, but broad enough to save it from being too Western or too cute. He especially disliked cute. And the narrow eyes with the strong, flaring eyebrows...he loved the look of those eyes, even now as she blinked them rapidly in an effort to awaken as fully as possible in a perhaps futile attempt to avoid the inevitable end.

She was conveniently half naked in sleep and as she responded to his gesture to stand, he could now see, pressing against a thin T-shirt, the well-formed breasts – she'd still been nursing Angelica – which, looking at her photo on the plane, he could only imagine. He was pleased to see that they weren't too large and fleshy like those of the many Western girls he had known in the hostess bars of Roppongi, or too tiny, like many Asian women's, despite the influence of cheeseburgers on the genetic inheritance of modern Japanese.

Even better, she had broad hips – no protruding hipbones like on so many of the Japanese bar girls – and an enticing rounding of the belly with a faint tracery of stretch marks, which only inflamed his desire to take her before killing her even more. So as she emerged from the bed sheets like a tragic Venus from a seashell of doom, Ohsanshouo made up his mind that he would indeed fuck Fumié Akahoshi before firing the final, fatal shot.

*   *   *

The surf was good at Todos Santos this week and when *Los Derechos del Hombre* finally docked at Puerto San Carlos and off-loaded its catch of albacora, bonito and dorado, Jorge Luis Valenzuela jumped on his Kawasaki Zephyr motorcycle and headed for the beach. Taking a late afternoon break in the bar after a couple hours in the waves, the Silver Surfer of Todos Santos learned from the bartender that the famous Japanese manga artist, the wife of his favorite comix artist Maxx Powers, and a lover who he never really expected to hear from again, was back in Todos Santos and was looking for him.

He decided to bide his time, to let her search a little before being allowed to find. Maybe the little flashing red light on his answering machine indicated a message from her which, in his haste to capture some good rides, he'd deliberately neglected to reveal.

So after a couple of *cervezas*, Jorge Luis Valenzuela, the Silver Surfer of Todos Santos, returned to his surfboard and his beach.

*   *   *

Back at the now separated couple's mansion in Den-en-chofu, Maxx Powers began to feel out his new role as a single dad with two young children, Bird and Angelica, to care for. Briefly, he entertained the idea of flying to his hideaway in Todos Santos, but quickly rejected any thoughts of going anywhere which might uncover Fumié's trail and make things easier for the *yakuza*. While, perhaps intuitively, he believed that Todos Santos was where Fumié would eventually end up, he didn't know for certain when this might be.

He likewise didn't know anything about Fumié's affair with the Silver Surfer nor that his daughter Angelica was actually the child of Jorge Luis Valenzuela, nor did he have any capacity to conceive the fantastic fact that Angelica Akahoshi, while not really his daughter, was actually his granddaughter since her father, the Silver Surfer of Todos Santos, was actually his son.

Next door to the Akahoshi/Powers residence, Mango Kamishita had also heard the gunshots in the night, and being the daughter of the late *yakuza* money launderer, Kenichi Kamishita, a highly valued associate of the Kurotombo-gumi organization, she immediately understood what was happening...a phone call to Junichiro Yamasaki. Yamasaki-san explained to her that the Right-wing "Commandant" Kuroyama, actually just a lowly junior high school principal, Takayama-*sensei*, in normal life, had paid a substantial fee to have the woman who insulted the Japanese Emperor in her comic book "taken care of." Kurotombo-gumi always honored their contracts. That was the nature of their business practice and the secret of their success. There could be no further negotiation on that point, he was sorry to say.

But as far as the children and the husband, the American Maxx Powers, well, they were of no interest to him or his organization. Kurotombo's international intelligence network would have little trouble tracking down an amateur fugitive. Taking children or foreigners hostage would only bring the police into the case, and as Mango herself was well aware, this was the last thing any *yakuza* crime boss wanted. The lines of division in Japan, as she herself so well knew, were clearly drawn – the *yakuza*, the Right-wingers, the ruling party, the major construction companies, the police, the Imperial Household Agency – they all had their roles, they all co-operated in keeping the country running smoothly, they all kept out of each other's way and avoided any official (and thereby traceable) connections as much as possible.

No, Yamasaki-san re-assured her, she didn't have to concern herself with the children's safety, but as far as her friend and neighbor Fumié Akahoshi, well, he was very sorry, but his hands were tied. There was nothing further that he could do.

But there was something that Mango Kamishita could do, and she wasted little time in doing it. Soon after she heard Fumié's Mercedes speed out of the neighborhood, she phoned Maxx Powers.

*   *   *

After he returned to his little white-washed casa from the beach, washed down his surfboard and took a quick shower, Jorge Luis Valenzuela pushed the little red button on his answering machine and for the first time in more than two years heard the voice of his former brief but brightly burning flame, Fumié Akahoshi, the rich Japanese woman and famous manga artist. The message was vague but urgent. There was an undertone of fear that he could pick up beneath the tone of forced calm in her voice. Although he couldn't have imagined the source of the fear, nor for that matter the motivation for this totally unexpected call, he decided that it might not be the best idea to play it cool after all.

So the Silver Surfer dressed quickly, pulling on his torn-at-the-knees blue jeans and his favorite *RanXerox* t-shirt, the bulging-muscled, goggle-eyed Italian comix cyborg raging mutely on a fading black background, and headed off on his Kawasaki to rendezvous with Fumié Akahoshi, a little surprised that she was staying at a rather modest little hotel off the beach and not at Maxx Powers' casa. He nearly ran over her wildly running toward him on a narrow, dusty road.

*　　　*　　　*

The Old Man decided to stay in his hotel room and watch his great-granddaughter Angelica Akahoshi's interview. Later that evening he would be meeting his sons, Maxx Powers and Ichiro, and Angelica at the Blue Note jazz club to listen to his grandson Bird Powers and his trio. Bird had been based in San Francisco for years now, but made regular tours to Tokyo, Hong Kong, Kuala Lumpur and other Asian cities. This would be the first reunion of the Old Man's extended family and, for all he knew, the last.

"Well, let's get back to your real Mom, your birth mother," the TV interviewer went on. "Fumié Akahoshi became a best-selling manga artist and one of Japan's richest women several years before you were born, but disappeared after publishing a highly controversial manga story which slandered the Japanese Emperor. You were just two years old at the time. Have I got that right so far?"

"Sorta...but the manga in question, *Chibi Hanako-chan in the 5th Dimension*, was obviously a fantasy...it all takes place in an alternative world...a parallel universe perhaps, but the parallel lines are warped, not straight. At most, it raised the very real question of a certain Japanese Emperor's involvement in a very real war crime – the rape and sexual enslavement of thousands of innocent women. You might recall a famous dialog balloon in the story where Chibi Hanako-chan says to Dorado-kun: 'Silence is the voice of complicity'."

*   *   *

"Hurry up and get on," said the Silver Surfer, stunned by the trembling of Fumié Akahoshi's body, as ominous as the slow trembling beneath the floorboards when a major earthquake foreshadows its awesome, world-shaking force, and by the sight of her half-naked body, clothed only in the T-shirt she'd slept in, a rare, hand-painted Polka Dot Demon by S. Clay Wilson, but totally unable to grasp the anonymous power which was the moment's source.

*   *   *

The TV interviewer, obviously very uncomfortable with the prospect of discussing Imperial guilt or responsibility before a national audience on the government-sponsored network, hastily changed the subject back to Angelica's first book, *Cloth Monkey*. The Old Man found the remote under the luggage stand and pumped up the volume.

"Going back to your surrogate mother, Mango Kamishita, with whom you lived for ten years before she was killed in a freak accident...."

"Wait a minute please. Mango was run down on the street on her way to my elementary school graduation ceremony. It was the first time that I knew of that she ever left her house. The night before she drew up my family tree for me...all the complicated relationships stemming from all the one-night stands. I never knew who my real father was while I was growing up, but I always felt much closer to Mango than to Maxx...I think all that's covered in *Cloth Monkey*. But to call her death a freak accident is a false assumption. There were three "eye-witness" reports to the local police box. They all called it a hit and run, but one said she was hit by a 'scooter chick' on a Yamaha Vino, another said it was a big foreigner on a mountain bike, and the third said it was a boy on a pizza delivery trike. The body was claimed by her 'uncle' from Adachi Ward and cremated the next day."

*   *   *

"*OK, turn around!*" Ohsanshouo ordered.

So, she thought, he was gonna shoot her in the back, in the back of the head most likely, so she turned slowly, reluctantly, hoping the end would come fast and without too much pain. She'd been hoping to distract him through eye contact, or to at least be able to read some sign of faint hope for her survival in his eyes. *Well, kiss all that goodbye.*

Ohsanshouo was enthralled by the sight of Fumié Akahoshi's pear-shaped ass. This was, to his eyes, a much better treat than the hipless "peach ass" of the typical Japanese bar girl. He made up his mind for good. "*OK, now bend over!*" he commanded.

*   *   *

Like millions of other TV viewers throughout Japan, the Old Man moved closer to the TV screen. This interview was obviously moving beyond the borders of the script.

"Another thing you probably remember from *Cloth Monkey* was the scene depicting the death of Mango's parents at the Pyramids. All the media reported the tragedy as a terrorist attack."

"That's right," Sato-san managed, trying to maintain her calm while losing control of the interview. "Muslim fundamentalists were trying to discourage tourism, which provided revenue for the secular government."

"Well, that's one story," Angelica countered. "But there are a few facts that maybe you should know. One is that Mango's father, Kamishita-san, was a money launderer for the Kurotombo-gumi crime organization, in other words, the *yakuza*. Another is that Kurotombo was engaged in a turf war at the time with a rival gang, the Koizumi-kai. A third is that the Kamishita's bodies were identified and recovered the next day by two 'uncles' from Adachi Ward, Tokyo – a Mr. Taito and a Mr. Setagaya. The bodies were flown back to Tokyo the same day and cremated. The name 'Kamishita' never appeared in any media reports along with those of the rest of the Japanese victims. Do you think that Muslim terrorists would go to all that trouble?"

"Maybe it's a bit suspicious," Sato-san, the interviewer, admitted.

"Well, there's one more fact to ponder...what can you tell me about the uncles' names – 'Taito' and 'Setagaya'?"

"Uh...wait a minute...I think I know...neither 'Taito' nor 'Setagaya' are included in the official Japanese registry of acceptable surnames?"

"Bingo!"

*   *   *

Fumié Akahoshi let the shudder pass over her, inhaling and exhaling as deep and slow as possible. This too, the rape, was not unexpected. But here too lay her one advantage, her pale glimmer of hope at the end of a long, dark cave. As she slowly opened her legs to ease the assault of her assassin, a plan formed in her mind, which had become as empty and focused as never before.

First, put the room in Alpha. As her left hand braced against the mattress of the bed, the thumb and first two fingers of her right hand came together, channeling all her psychic energy into one point. As her breathing slowed and steadied and the cycles per second of neuro-electrical energy in her brain decreased and entered into the realm of psychic power, Fumié felt Ohsanshouo also relax, felt the anger and aggression leaving his body which was now able to savor the pleasure he had up until now only dreamed of.

He entered her easily, much more easily than he expected. She pushed her hips back against his bulk and concentrated on contacting the muscles of her vagina to hold him close. Absurdly, one of the Old Man's silly baseball sayings echoed in the empty chambers of her mind...*anything can happen if you put the ball in play.*

*   *   *

"So just to recap and bring us up to your new book, your latest graphic novel, Mango Kamishita named you as her sole heir in her will, so besides her house, the house you grew up in, you also inherited a considerable fortune. Then, the next year, when *Cloth Monkey* won the Akutagawa Prize, you, at the ripe age of thirteen, became famous as well as rich. And now that Fumié Akahoshi has been declared legally dead, you've inherited the bulk of her fortune as well. Yet before you reached your teens you'd already lost both your birth mother and your surrogate mother. How do you feel about these extremes of fortune and misfortune in your life?"

"I think you'll have to read my new book to get the answer to that."

The Old Man turned down the volume of the TV. He had not yet read Angelica's new graphic novel – she was to give him a signed copy tonight at the Blue Note. But he did read the many letters that Fumié had sent him in the years between her marriage to Maxx Powers and her disappearance in Mexico a few years later.

A lot of the letters spoke of her friendship with the recluse Mango Kamishita.

He remembered especially her descriptions of Mango's world inside her spacious mansion. And Mango, it seemed, had a love life, with her martial arts instructor who visited regularly and taught both Mango and Fumié, who had practiced karate in the mandatory martial arts program at her junior high school, in the elaborate dojo that Mango had commissioned on the ground floor, with sliding glass doors facing out to the magnificent walled garden. The instructor, who Fumié never referred to as anything other than "Kung Fu," spent many of his off-duty hours in the garden. And if the second story balcony was Mango's border town, the walled garden was the border town of Kung Fu.

Maxx, she wrote to him, was not interested in martial arts, but he loved the sea. He kept a fiberglass day-sailor at Kamakura and a slightly larger cruising sloop in Todos Santos and had taught Fumié the rudiments of sailing. Fumié guessed that in his own way he was still trying to put together the puzzle of his surrogate father Max Roach's disappearance.

The Old Man turned the volume back up just as the interview was wrapping up. The last words he heard Angelica Akahoshi say were these: "...and I'll tell you one more thing...this leather jacket sure is heavy."

*   *   *

Typically, sex lasted no longer for Ohsanshouo than the average sumo match. A few seconds, a minute or two at most, and it was climatically and decisively over. Time to bow out and leave the arena.

With her mind still and relentlessly centered, Fumié saw the glint of gunmetal lean away from her, toward the open window, felt the pre-ejaculatory stiffening and locking of the engorged entity deep inside her and instantly made her move, all the accumulated karate and kung fu practice recalled and articulated, joining forces with the Alpha mind control power willing her to survive and escape.

First, a twisting, lightning fast kick in the balls of her attacker, rapidly followed by the most powerful rabbit chop to the back of the massive neck that her lightweight body, aided by a huge dose of adrenaline, could deliver, and completed by an almost simultaneous knee to Ohsanshouo's notoriously glass chin. The giant fell, knees on the floor, upper body slumped on the bed. Then, she threw the gun out the open window into the foliage below and fled.

*   *   *

"Just relax," the Silver Surfer said to her, inanely. But there was a spark of truth hidden in this flinty banality: "He's got nothing to connect you with me...and besides, you're getting out of here right away."

The Kawasaki Zephyr's 750cc engine rumbled confidently through the night up the back roads toward Puerto San Carlos. Sitting behind him, as close and tight as humanly possible, her ear and cheek pressed against his neck, Fumié Akahoshi could both feel and hear the Silver Surfer's voice as he laid out his plan.

There was a small yacht, *Spindrift*, a 30' catamaran, anchored in a hidden cove south of Puerto San Carlos. The owners, an American couple from Santa Barbara, had coasted down in her and were now off for a week's holiday in Torreon, to celebrate their landing and "to get as far from the sea as possible and still be in Mexico."

He, Jorge Luis, had told them about this fairly isolated spot, since they wanted to avoid having to pay moorage fees at a wharf in the harbor. The anchors were heavy, but he'd help her haul them up. He assumed that since her husband Maxx had a sailboat, a 28' sloop, and since he'd seen her at the helm while out sailing with him, that she could reasonably handle the cat single-handed in the Northeast Trades.

Fumié gasped, but the rumble of the engine probably drowned it out.

The yacht was well stocked with food and water. Even though it was small enough for a solo sailor to handle, it was big enough for the ocean in these latitudes and at this time of year. And, it was fast! If necessary, she could reach Hawaii in 10 days.

*   *   *

After graduating from a prestigious international high school in Tokyo, Angelica Akahoshi set off to find her mother, Fumié and her father, Jorge Luis Valenzuela, the Silver Surfer of Todos Santos. She spent several years among the young global trekkers and back-packers, surfers and snowboarders, drug smugglers and mercenaries. Although rich and famous in Japan, she met no one in her travels who'd ever heard of the Akutagawa Prize or read her graphic novel *Cloth Monkey*. But every now and then, on some sun saturated tropical beach or dank, grim mountain hostel or back alley of some major European or South American capital, she would hear the rumors...the stories...the legend.

It was never quite the same as the last time she heard it. The locations were always different, the characters often different ages, of different nationalities. No one had ever actually met them or seen them in person...they had a friend.... But at least once every year, sometimes more than that, tales of a strange couple, an ageless woman, Asian or Inuit or west coast American Indian, a younger man, handsome, taciturn, wearing a colorful headscarf, riding an antiquated long board, always on the outer edges of the beach. The woman was said to be a healer, someone who could cure illness and injury with a method something like reiki, using both her hands and her mind.

For a while she followed the trails...Puerto Bolivar, Ecuador, near the border with Peru...Uribia, Columbia, near the border with Venezuela...St. Georges, French Guiana, on the border with Brazil....even Viana do Castelo, Portugal, near the Spanish border and Khota Bharu, Malaysia, on the Thai frontier. Always small coastal border towns...always a trail run cold.

So finally she returned to Tokyo, to Den-en-chofu. She lived, alone, or with an occasional boyfriend (they averaged about three months) in the mansion she'd inherited from her surrogate mother, Mango Kamishita, and worked, always alone, creating her own version of the story in the studio of her long-lost birth mother, Fumié Akahoshi, in the other mansion she was soon to inherit next door.

*   *   *

Ohsanshouo slowly recovered from his swift, painful and totally unexpected beating. He was big and tough, if not much else. But he was smart enough to know that his career as a hit man for the Kurotombo-gumi was down the toilet unless he could get another chance at the woman, the comic book artist, he'd been paid to kill. And, even worse, he realized someone would probably soon be paid to kill him.

Ohsanshouo was also enough of a thinker to repress a panic-driven mad search which could only make his chance for a second chance even worse. No...cool, relaxed, professional...that was the way to act. He would have to act the role of a tourist as best he could, to get the information he needed to locate his target once again. And no monkey business.

His best bet was to get in with the young locals hanging around the beach, because they would be the most informed concerning the local gossip, the most naïve, and the most likely to talk about what they knew. So he would begin his hunt down at the beach soon, as dawn was breaking, doing what he loved most in life, surfing.

* * *

A couple of days after his first conversation with Shomer ben Ghoshi, the Israeli mafia lawyer phoned him back... and with a set of instructions – "no questions and no stalling, get it?" Maxx Powers got it. He drove to the appointed address in Adachi Ward, Tokyo and was met and escorted into a rather ordinary looking office in a nondescript concrete low-rise.

There were two men in the office when he was pushed in by his escorts. The older one was conservatively dressed in a gray suit, white shirt and pale green tie, while the younger was a bit flashier, but by no means sartorially over the top. The younger man introduced himself as "Mr. Bunkyo" and his obvious superior as "Mr. Chuo." Maxx bowed several times, probably deeper than was necessary.

Without wasting time, Mr. Bunkyo gave Maxx two envelopes – a thin one, which held a round trip ticket to La Paz, Mexico, the closest airport to Todos Santos – and a thick one, which contained a bundle of American dollars.

* * *

The Old Man turned off the TV, put on his jacket and walking shoes and left the hotel. He walked to Shinjuku

Station, caught the Yamanote train to Shibuya where he changed to the Tokyu Toyoko train bound for Yokohama, kept his seat as the train went underground for its stop at Den-en-chofu and got off two stops further on in Shin Maruko. From there he walked for about 20 minutes until he reached the Tamagawa River and Baseball Beach.

The river was running fast and the estuarian tide was high and still rising. The Old Man built a small fire with driftwood and sat before it cradling in his hands a rubber baseball he'd picked up at the tideline. These were the elements – the river, the baseball, the flames – to carry him back to the past.

The old friends that Ichiro was hanging around with in Tokyo were his Little League teammates from over 30 years ago. The Old Man had been their coach. His three rules had produced a club which committed surprisingly few errors for their age group, and his philosophy, combined with their natural enthusiasm and modest athletic talents, had brought them into the Kanagawa Prefecture Little League finals. They had just barely won the Nakahara Ward title, and then, bursting with confidence and a well-deserved sense of accomplishment, took the Kawasaki city crown and went on to the Prefectural tournament.

Their opponent was Yokohama's Naka Ward, who boasted one of the most powerful Little League pitchers in Japan. Eleven-year-old Tetsuya Satozaki had pitched three shutouts in a row, topped off by a perfect game in the semi-final match against the powerful team of young rice farmers' sons from Hiratsuka.

The Naka Ward batters were no slouches either and they tagged the international team's American born pitcher Joey Piersall for three runs in the first inning. Although the internationals couldn't do much against Satozaki, Piersall also settled down and kept Yokohama off the scoreboard for the next three innings.

But Yokohama's slugger Go Watanabe hit a homer with a runner on in the top of the fifth and four straight singles off Venezuelan born reliever Juan Comacho in the sixth and last inning brought home two more runs and pretty much put the game out reach. The Old Man's boys had put only three runners on base so far, on singles in the third and fourth innings and a walk in the bottom of the fifth.

Bobby Kato, the international's shortstop, led off the last inning with an opposite field single to right, stole second on the very next pitch and went to third on pinch hitter Takeshi Engelbert's sacrifice fly. That brought up the Old Man's son, Ichiro.

*   *   *

Spindrift's stern anchor was the heavier and since there was no winch to assist them, they were winded after hauling it on board. "Let's go down and look at the chart," Jorge Luis suggested. Fumié was only too happy to agree.

The starboard cabin had a pull-down chart table with a chart of Baja California Sur in place. The Silver Surfer ushered his distressed lover over to it, grabbed a set of calipers and parallel rules from a nearby tray, and wasted no time explaining the plan.

"OK, you'll be leaving as soon as we get the sails set and the bow anchor up. The prevailing winds are northwesterly right now, so once out of the cove, head South, on the broad reach. You'll intersect the Tropic of Cancer sometime tomorrow...there's a Sat/Nav...over here. Turn it on just at sunrise tomorrow morning and keep an eye on it. You can spend a lot of time in the cabin because she self-steers well if you tie off the wheel by a spoke once you're on course. I assume you can read a compass? Good. Oh, and don't use any other electronics. They've got the engine key. It's a diesel, so you can't hot wire it. And without the engine you can't charge up the batteries for the electronics."

With the stern anchor up, the catamaran turned to the ebbing tide, the tide which Fumié would use to take her out of the cove.

"So, when you hit the T of C, head East. You'll be on a beam reach and the port hull might lift if it gets gusty, so put on a life-line harness and strap it to the rail...you'll be in the trough and it could get shaky if the waves build up high. This boat goes really fast and you could never catch it if you went overboard."

Fumié took three deep breaths and began to will herself to calm down, to put the cabin, the boat, herself, in Alpha. Her thumb and forefingers came together in her familiar focusing gesture.

"You should see me in 24 hours. If you don't, head for Hawaii. OK, *vamanos!* Let's go! *Ikimashou!*"

"*Gambarimasu!*" Fumié added. "*Vamanos! Ikimashou!*"

*   *   *

The Old Man tossed the hard rubber baseball up and caught it a few times, all the while sitting on a small drift-wood stump before the fire. He remembered that he'd called Ichiro over and whispered a plan in his ear. Ichiro'd nodded, turned and ran to home plate. Bobby Kato danced off third. He was one of the best runners on the team. On the first pitch, Ichiro faked a bunt. Strike one. The infielders edged closer to the plate.

Ichiro swung hard at the next pitch and hit a vicious one-hopper back at the pitcher's mound. Bobby Kato was zooming down the third base line. Yokohama's pitcher Satozaki, charging in expecting a squeeze bunt, was caught on the chest by the bouncing ball, but recovered in time to throw Ichiro out at first. But not before Kato had come home. Score: 7-1.

If this were a Hollywood movie or an inspirational story in a manga or on Japanese TV, the foreigners would have made a game of it, milking the melodrama to either defeat or victory by a single run. But the Old Man's memory of this event ran true. The next batter, Barry Esposito, son of the Nicaraguan Cultural Attaché, went after Satozaki's fastball and popped it up between second and third. The shortstop called it, made a routine catch and the game, as well as the season, were over for the Old Man's team. Ichiro found little consolation, at the time, in having driven in the lone run scored against Satozaki in the tournament. "We lost," he said, stone-faced. "I made an out."

＊　　　　＊　　　　＊

Angelica Akahoshi spent two years writing and drawing her story of what became of her parents. She gradually became closer to her brother Bird and to her grandfather, Maxx Powers. Close enough for her to be the one to reveal to Maxx the fact that Jorge Luis Valenzuela and not he, Maxx Powers, was her real father and, more shocking still, that Maxx was indeed the Silver Surfer's father...and her grandfather.

And close enough for Maxx to reveal to her the facts of

his mission to La Paz. Maxx had been met at the airport by the same two men who had escorted him up to Mr. Chuo's office in Adachi Ward, Mr. Taito and Mr. Setagaya. They again escorted him, this time to a large central police building, where he was relieved of his burden of American dollars. Messers Taito and Setagaya, meanwhile, went off to Todos Santos to identify and claim the body of Ohsanshouo, the big sumo wrestler, whose mother, so they said, was Mr. Taito's sister. The details of the corpse's cremation the next day in Tokyo are perhaps best left un-described.

The official police report of the incident in Todos Santos described the following events:

1) A visiting surfer, one Ika Nanao Moana, a.k.a. Ohsanshouo, was attacked by a tiger shark while on his board and killed. Cause of death – blood loss.

2) A local surfer, one Jorge Luis Valenzuela, a.k.a. the Silver Surfer, heroically swam out to warn the visitor that a shark had been spotted. His body has never been found and it is assumed he was eaten by the shark. His short board was found washed up on the beach.

3) A regular visitor, one Fumié Akahoshi, a.k.a. "the rich Japanese woman," has gone missing. Her passport was found in the cabin of the American catamaran yacht *Spindrift* which was found drifting in the sea off Cabo San Lucas. This case is unsolved and an investigation will soon be undertaken.

4) An eyewitness reports having seen "the rich Japanese woman," half-naked, running out of a hotel and "a giant Hawaiian or Samoan" leaving the same hotel a few hours later. It was also learned that the rich Japanese woman's husband kept a casa in Todos Santos, but that she was not, apparently, staying there.

Capitan Santana, the police officer in charge of the Todos

Santos affair, handed Maxx Fumié Akahoshi's passport. He held Maxx's eye for a moment and then winked. "A lovers' quarrel, no?"

* * *

Angelica Akahoshi's graphic novel *Border Town* begins with the meeting on the Tropic of Cancer. The sun is setting on the ocean's horizon and a mosaic of rose and mauve rises from just above the surface of the sea, while autumnal orange slashed with an ominous gray reaches into the darkening sky. A flash of beetle green undercuts the entire image. The catamaran is tiny, just a few strokes of the pen, in black. The shadow of the mountain range along the coastline is nothing more than an inky blur.

The boat is the focus of the next panel, and the surfer and his long board are approaching it in the foreground. In the next frame, the woman is helping him climb aboard.

For many pages after this, the extreme peril of the voyage of a thousand miles unfolds. Although beginning hopefully with the selection of the few essentials transferred from boat to board – two canvas sun-hats, plastic jugs of water, a knife & whetstone, a spool of fishing line & some hooks – and the donning of the dry-suits, the story gradually descends into despair.

First, the unrelenting sun, the drinking of each other's urine after their water runs out, the arm-weariness of the surfer when the westerlies drop and the sea falls flat. Finally, rain, the replenishing of their water supply – at least for a while.

For a few days and pages, hope returns. There is the capture of a big dorado, its iridescent rainbow colored scales flashing in a benevolent sun as it leaps, trying desperately to shake the hook. There is a fantastic scene of the woman cutting sashimi from the big fish and the couple toasting each other with water, sitting cross-legged on the surfboard, feasting, as once again the sun goes down in the west.

There is one full-page dramatic drawing of the surfer skillfully riding the blue water swells, the woman's arms entwining his body, straight and solid as a mast. Then, inevitably, the tropical storm with its dark skies and towering waves, the humans reduced to pitiful, cringing lumps of black neoprene-encased flesh, lashed to the board with rope, the knots meticulously painted by the artist.

At last, a Guatemalan landfall is made. And here the real adventure begins.

*　　　　　*　　　　　*

Surfing was the one passion shared by Ika Nanao Moana, the ex-sumo wrestler Ohsanshouo and would-be *yakuza* hitman, and Jorge Luis Valenzuela, the Silver Surfer of Todos Santos. Perhaps their attraction to Fumié Akahoshi was another, although the perverse lust of the one stood in stark contrast to the loving devotion of the other.

Tourists were nothing new on the beaches of Todos Santos, but the presence of the huge Japanese-Samoan with the outlandish mix of Maori, Japanese and Celtic tattoos caused all but the most dedicated of the local surfers, out for the early morning break, to turn their heads, at least one time, for a second look. The Silver Surfer, however, didn't need a second look, as the giant paddled his rented board out into the swells. Then, he too paddled out into the waves and spent an uneventful morning surfing...and watching.

Ohsanshouo, after emerging from the surf, spent the rest of the morning cultivating camaraderie with a group of young hotshots among the regular local surfers. The Silver Surfer casually observed all of this, but without too much concern, since he knew that none of the hotshots knew anything about his connection with the rich Japanese woman, or even the fact that the day before she had been back in town. He figured that sooner or later the hit-man would be in the bars, probing for information.

Later in the day, Jorge Luis Valenzuela secretly followed Ohsanshouo back to his hotel, and while the big sumotori had his nap, he returned to the beach and spread the word among his friends, hanging out in the cool of the seaside cantinas, waiting for the evening break that everyone should get out of the water a half hour before sunset — there was going to be a shark in the water. Then, Jorge Luis returned to his casa and sat in his white-walled kitchen honing the blade of his razor-thin fish knife. He paid special attention to sharpening the serrated top of the blade, normally used to flay the scales off of fish.

Late in the afternoon, the Silver Surfer, skirting the populated stretch of beach, paddled his short board along the edge of treed shoreline which ran at a right angle to the beach, towing his old Hawaiian long board behind him. When he came to a section of mangrove, he stopped, tied the long board to a protruding mangrove root, and slowly angled back toward the surf.

*　　　*　　　*

Death came suddenly and unexpectedly, like a shark attack, to Ohsanshouo.

Slipping off his board and swimming silently, mostly under-water, Jorge Luis Valenzuela approached his target as dusk obscured the clarity of the scene at sea. As ex-*Komusubi* Ohsanshouo sat astride his surfboard waiting for a building set of waves, one swift stroke of a razor-sharp fish knife severed the Great Saphenous Vein of his massive left leg, just behind the knee, rendering him helpless and bleeding profusely. Then, the clean, deadly wound was mangled by the sharpened scaler of the Silver Surfer's blade. And as the doomed Ohsanshouo struggled mightily but hopelessly toward the beach, Jorge Luis Valenzuela, the Silver Surfer of Todos Santos, swam far out into the Pacific Ocean and let the murder weapon drop from his revengeful hand and fall the many forgetful fathoms to the bottom.

finis

Shichifukujin (Seven Lucky Gods)
illustrations by Taeko Onitsuka

New Orphic Publishers

706 Mill Street, Nelson, B.C. V1L 4S5 Canada
Fax: 250-353-0743 E-mail: neworphic 1@hotmail.com

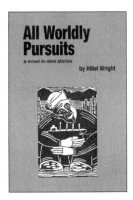

With luminous and articulate writing, Wright tells the story of Wiley Moon. He has a lust for life and a passion that involves the reader in his story.
—W.P. Kinsella, author of *Shoeless Joe*

Wright mananges to spin a narrative line taut enough to keep us turning the pages.
—David Cozy, *Kyoto Journal*

To this reader the best stories out of the 38 are "The Invisible Lover," in which a Chinese girl makes love with an invisible man (a concept of genius), and the wonderful title story, in which a man recollects his entire existence in between the rituals of eating sushi.
—Colin Donald, *The Daily Yomiuri*, Tokyo

Rotary Sushi has the special merit and charm of an original mind capable of coping with matters that are grave and constant . . . it will appeal to all who admire intelligent rebellion.
—Bob Williams, author of *Joyce Country*

Distributed in Japan by Intercontinental Marketing Corporation
http://imcbook.net
Distributed in USA by SARU Press International
http://sarupress.org
Distributed world-wide by Printed Matter Press
http://www.printedmatterpress.com

New from Printed Matter Press

The Snake that Bowed
by Edward Seidensticker
Novel, 160 pages, Paperback
ISBN 1-933606-03-7
US $15.00, ¥1,575

A View from the Chuo Line and other stories by Donald Richie
Short stories, 128 pages, Paperback
ISBN 0-965330-46-X
US $15.00, Yen 1,575

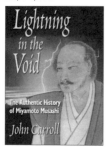

Lightning in the Void: The Authentic History of Miyamoto Musashi by John
Carroll, Novel, 528 pages, Paperback
ISBN 1-933606-02-9
US $25.00, ¥2,500

She said . . .
by Aileen Fedullo
Poetry 108 pages, Paperback with CD
ISBN 1-933606-04-5
US $15.00, ¥1,575

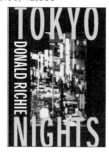

Tokyo Nights by Donald Richie
Novel, 224 pages, Paperback
ISBN 1-933606-00-2
US $15.00, ¥1,575

Nines by Michel Englebert
Poetry, 64 pages, Paperback
ISBN 1-933606-09-6
US $10.00, ¥1,050

Green Tea to Go: Stories from Tokyo
by Leza Lowitz, 180 pages, Paperback
ISBN 0-935086-32-3
US $15.00, ¥1,575

Companions of the Holiday
by Donald Richie, novel, 192 pages,
Paperback ISBN 1-933606-06-1
US $15.00, ¥1,575

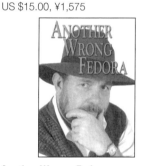

Another Wrong Fedora
by John Gribble
Poetry, 120 pages, Paperback
ISBN 1-933606-01-0
US $15.00, ¥1,575

Fair Play: Behind the Scenes of Sports Marketing by Jack Sakazaki
Autobiography, 176 pages, Paperback,
ISBN 1-933606-07-X
US $15.00, ¥1,575

Printed Matter Press Books

Order directly from PMP

Printed Matter Press
Yagi Bldg. 4F, 2-10-13 Shitaya, Taito-ku
Tokyo 110-0004, Japan

390 Mason Avenue
Staten Island,
New York 10305

http://www.printedmatterpress.com

PMP Books are distributed in Japan by Yohan Inc.
and are available at or through all major foreign bookstores.

about the author

Hillel Wright has lived in Hawaii, mainland USA and Canada and now lives in Japan with wife and Muse Shiori Tsuchiya.

about the Muse

Shiori Tsuchiya has lived in Canada and Japan. She is author of two books of poetry written in English, *Screaming Soul* and *Here/Hear I Am*.

about the artist

Taeko Onitsuka was born in 1972, likes to draw and lives in Gifu Prefecture, Japan.